Set in 1959, this Jo Murphy Mystery introduces Doctor Jo Murphy a pathologist and General Practitioner who lived in Clapham. This is her adventure as told by her mentor and friend Richard Regan.

Murder on Cedars Road

By

Michael Fitzalan

Copyright © 2017 by Michael Fitzalan

Dedication

To mothers and fathers, brothers, sisters, husbands, wives, sons and daughters.

Murder on Cedars Road

Murder on Cedars Road is a Jo Murphy Mystery

By

Michael Fitzalan

Contents

Chapter One – The Man – Mars the Bringer of War

The man was wearing a balaclava, not one of those open faced woollen ones that everyone used to wear to keep warm in winter, but a menacing black mask with just two holes for the eyes and a slit for the mouth. Jo wished she had been dressed for flying; her green *Pierre Balmain* skirt suit was not ideal for fight or flight. They were matched in height, he was six foot; Jo was tall, five foot nine. Being on the third floor of number one Wetherby Gardens meant the window could not provide escape.

She flicked, her long blonde hair away from her face, trying to see what colour her assailant's eyes were, trying to see if she recognised them. They stared at her, ice blue like her own, but his burned with anger while hers searched the room for something with which she could defend herself. A knife-wielding thug threatened her on the other side of the desktop.

He had the power: he had the strength. He was militarily fit; he was a soldier or a physical training instructor. Her long limbs might allow her to outrun him but he was beefy.

She looked on, as her attacker approached; he hunched his shoulders, preparing to pounce; his black bomber jacket made him look even bigger than he was. He was a bear of a man. A knife was in his right hand, the other hand made a grab for her. She dodged out of the way, finding momentary sanctuary behind the desk in the corner of the room. She placed her hands on the green leather top, ready to spring to the left or the right depending on the side he chose.

Tweed had been disturbed, she noticed his black backpack on the desk, next to it the papers he was meant to be stealing and his black leather gloves, which he had taken off to handle the sheaves. She had no idea what he was looking for and if he got hold of her she would never know. I had been a mistake to come up here alone but then she had expected to find the flat empty.

Survival was her only concern. The investigation could wait.

She weighed up her chances, noticed how long thighs his looked in his tight fitting trousers, she recognised them as ski-pants, he would definitely be able to run faster than her, she was wearing a skirt.

The stirrup hidden by his brown Jodhpur boots, she wondered if they might have a steel toecap and vowed to watch for any kicks he might make.

Her assailant could crush her with his strength. She might be able to outrun him. All her emotions screamed at her to get away before he killed her.

Desperately, she grabbed the table lamp on the desk and toyed with the idea of racing him around the bureau until they collapsed with exhaustion, she had been a phenomenal runner at medical school. Instead, she attacked. She knew her survival depended on it.

With a furious yank she pulled the flex from the socket, the wire whipped the back of her leg but she ignored the pain, pulling the flex up and bunching it around the base with her free hand. She waved the lamp in his face all the while. The lips, pouting through the slit of the balaclava, broke into a cruel closed mouth smile. She smiled back, showing her teeth in an ironic salutation, a sarcastic smile.

She poked the table lamp at his face. He tried to swat it away like a fly but each time she withdrew. Remembering her fencing lessons, she jabbed forward and moved back in a rhythmical dance, teasing him with the prospect of being hit by the heavy brass lamp stand. Fed up with her theatricals, he grabbed for the lamp. She allowed him to seize it.

Too late, he realised that he had grabbed the bulb. Quickly, she moved into action, putting both hands over his. She fastened his hand onto the burning orb, gripping his fist and wrist to keep it closed. She smelt searing flesh.

Roaring loudly, he dropped the knife from his right hand while he tried to move his other hand and wriggle free. She had trapped it securely. Any twisting and turning by him was matched by her.

"Take that you great Amadán," she hissed, holding his hand in place as he wriggled in her grasp. He pulled his arm away but she just followed, the pain in his hand was overwhelming and all he wanted to do was release the burning globe   that scorched his hand.

The burning became deeper, the longer he held the bulb. He was focused only on his pain, the burning sensation in his left hand. Finally, giving up on twisting free; he, instantly, brought up his free hand to push her away. She blocked the trajectory with her body foreseeing his clumsy attempts to relieve his pain.

Next, he tried to grab for the stem of the lamp using his right hand. He was not thinking straight but she was, she released her grip and gave him the lamp, kicking the knife across the floor at the same time; the blade slipped under a closed door and lodged there.

Holding his damaged hand above his head, to keep it away from danger, he backed away from her holding the lamp stand in his hand, not as an instrument of assault but a weapon to protect his other hand should she try and grab for it.

He realised it was an Achilles heel. All her instincts told her that this would be a fight to the death if she were not careful. Whether he was feigning defeat or he was actually afraid of what she might do next did not matter a jot to her; she had to act quickly and decisively, stopping him getting the knife and pushing home her slight advantage.

The odds were now in her favour. She had to use the advantage to prevent her attacker grabbing the knife again. If she failed, the consequences could be fatal.

She rushed forward, as he edged backwards towards the knife handle, brushing the lampstand and his undamaged hand away and before he could raise it to strike her, she planted her kneecap in the soft mass in his ski pants, not twice but thrice.

Groaning in pain, he collapsed on the floor releasing the lamp and curling into a ball. He tried to kick out, but Jo had stepped away. He was clearly not going to give up easily and nor was she. For good measure, she stomped on the burnt hand with her high heal, which made him cry out in pain and frustration, a gurgling scream that sounded horrific. As a doctor, inflicting pain rather than healing people baulked but she nevertheless felt he deserved punishment.

She knew he would be out of action for enough time for her to grab the knife and flee.

Without hesitation, she slipped over to the door bending down to extract and to retrieve the knife lodged under the bedroom door leaf.

Picking it up by the blade, she hurried to the hall door while slipping the knife handle first, into her coat pockets as she went.

The smashed telephone would offer her no help; she ran for the front door, grabbing the keys from his jacket that was hung on the door. Fumbling hurriedly for the keys, she saw him struggle to his knees, holding the wrist of his damaged hand.

Still nursing his injured hand, he leant on his elbows as he rose; his head lifted and she saw the pain etched on his face. The fire in his eyes burned even greater, she had never seen anyone so angry before. Jo extracted the keys from the left hand pocket and made a mental note, he had held his knife in his right hand but it appeared he would have transferred it to the left before using it.

Without meaning to, she had damaged his killing hand. It was the closest she had ever come to being stabbed but she was not going to stay around to heal him.

Wrenching open the front door, she slipped through it, slammed the door against the jamb and turning the brass key firmly in the mortise lock she fastened the door, locking it from the outside. All was quiet on the landing. None of the other flats had heard the struggle or if they had, they were staying firmly behind their closed doors. She assumed many of the occupants were away for the weekend or out; no wonder Tweed had felt able to burgle the flat number five.

She used the longer silver key to secure the brass escutcheon lock, too, for good measure. Jo reasoned that he would not be desperate enough to throw himself from a third floor flat. Extracting the keys, she popped them into her left hand pocket with the knife, adding to her collection. A cursory look into the common parts stairwell showed her the coast looked clear.

Swiftly, she descended the stairs, trotting down them, her left hand on the bannister rail, her right hand fishing for her own car keys.

Her leather shoes made no sound on the thick red carpet on the steps but clicked noisily on the marble floor as she dashed for the front door. She had signed the Hippocratic oath and yet for the first time she had hurt rather than healed a fellow human being. It bothered her. However, almost being murdered bothered her more. It was the third attempt in as many weeks. Outside, the darkness was lit by streetlights, the cold air hit her and she realised that she was perspiring.

There were three cars in the street, a *Commer* van, a *Ford Anglia* and a 1955, *Rolls Royce Silver Cloud,* registration *GPF 521*. She had left the door unlocked and, seizing the chrome handle, she pressed the button into the handle and opened the driver's door. Stepping in through the large door, she settled into the red leather seats before shutting the aluminium alloy door softly behind her. Inhaling the familiar leather smell, she took a deep and stilled her heart.

The mirrors revealed a deserted street behind her and ahead the road was clear, few people venturing out on a sombre Sunday evening. Slowly, she slipped the key into the dashboard to the left of the steering wheel and turned it to the right. The five litre, six cylinder purred into life and Jo selected drive from the stalk jutting from the left hand side of the steering column. Releasing the handbrake and raising her foot from the brake pedal, she took a brief look over her right shoulder before pressing down on the accelerator, the two-tone, brown beast moved into the night, travelling towards Hereford Square. She tick-tacked through the side streets, past Gloucester Road tube station and right on to the Cromwell Road, heading for Knightsbridge.

Within minutes the flat was a mile away. Jo settled into the driver's seat, staring ahead at the road, searching the pavements, her heart pounded in her chest, but her breathing was returning to normal. Adrenaline coursed through her body. She was more alert than she had ever been.

Her mind raced, processing what she had been through, the shock of the attack affected her emotions but her logical mind was already searching for solutions. She would need help. Pulling up outside a public phone box, a red Gilbert Scott design, she locked the car this time and scurried to the phone box.

Lifting the receiver, pushing a penny into the slot, she rapidly inserted her finger into the metal ring that danced around the figures as she dialled: 2-2-8-7-9-9-0. It took an eternity for the phone to be answered. When the call was picked up, she pressed button 'A'.

"George, I have a few things for you to take care of, can you send an ambulance and the police to 48 Wetherby Gardens, please," she whispered when she heard her husband say hello.

"I've a pen and paper handy," George answered in his soothing west coast brogue.

Chapter Two – i - Josephine and George

That was her story, which she related to me at Lyons' Corner House in The Strand. I travelled up from Maple Road, Penge in my gunship grey *Morris Minor 1000 Series* and she travelled up from the west side of Clapham in the Brown and beige *Rolls*. We parked in Craven Passage, which we had agreed over the telephone and walked to the restaurant opposite Charing Cross Station; it was the 10th June 1960.

Jo was pregnant but she did not show yet, it was a bit parky anyway and she was wearing her green thick wool overcoat over a tan skirt suit from *Jaeger*, I wore a sombre suit, a de-mob suit in slate grey from Burton.

So why was she telling me about all this? It's because I am a copper. My name is Richard Regan, people called me Dick in those days, the fifties; it was an acceptable nickname.

So why am I telling the story, now? The safety of years, which means most of the protagonists are dead, now. I was only 27 when I made Detective Inspector. I wanted to write about Jo before now but after typing so many reports, sitting at an *Olivetti* in the seventies, the effort of typing our story lasted less than a week. Rheumatism and the Rotary Club kept me away from the keys. So I am dictating this to my grandson Rory and he's my stenographer, a speed-typing journalist, he deserves a mention. He calls me Ricky or Rick.

Back at the Lyons teas house Jo finally got to tell me the denouement of our investigation. The Criminal Investigation Department had arrested the last of the Tweed twins and I was transferred to Division when I was promoted so our meeting was the first chance to hear the story from the horse's mouth.

Since our adventure, she had been working hard at her surgery and helping her husband to build up their pub portfolio so a Saturday lunch was the only time we could make for each other.

The children had gone to the *RAC* for a swim while George had a sauna; he practically lived in the Royal Automobile Club when he was not working.

She took me back to that night, telling me about facing Geoff Tweed and his knife.

"You must have been petrified," I exclaimed, looking in awe at this elegant lady who had escaped one of the Tweed twins, two notorious thugs in their day.

She was three months pregnant but she did not look it, good tailoring, and her height, her slimness, all helped. She turned quite a few heads in the restaurant.

The rumble of trolleys laden with cakes, the click of waitresses laying heavy cutlery and the clash and clack of tables being cleared became a background sound as we talked about that night; the night when the caper came to a close.

"I didn't have time to be frightened," she drawled in her cut glass Kensington voice, she was in no hurry.

She was a dichotomy, she told me, she had been born in the East End and yet she sounded like a resident of South Kensington.

"How come you talk even more posh than Queen and yet you told me you were cockney?" I asked.

I knew her well enough by now.

"I think you have fallen into the trap of preconception, surely you should be interested in inspection?" she replied cleverly, offering me a *Senior Service* cigarette.

"Well you could knock me down with a feather, you say you were born in a pub, sounds like you were born with a silver spoon in your mouth," I confessed, putting my hand up to decline the cigarette, " I thought you were giving up, that's the third one since you arrived."

"Cutting down, darling, cutting down."

"Not from where I am standing."

We both laughed, hers was care free and tinkled like crystal, mine was repressed Hendon. I knew that she called everyone darling; I was not going to get my hopes up. It still made me feel special despite myself. Logic and the heart are not good related, sadly.

"How's the toddler?" she asked, in those days infant mortality was high, it wasn't the halcyon days that everyone imagines.

No one believed what Super Mac told us that *we had never had it so good*. There was still a lot of poverty and ill-health around.

"He's on fine form after the whooping cough, my wife Susie is exhausted, after six weeks of it," I confessed.

"Pertussis is very nasty, you got off lightly. It can last ten weeks, I'm glad he's better. Make sure you give him plenty of milk and fish to build up his stamina."

"How are your brood?"

"All well, Heidi is looking after them, George is meeting me at the obstetricians."

"Have you thought of any names?" I ventured, hoping she might want to call the baby Richard, after me.

"Deidre or Fiona if it's a girl, Anton if it's a boy."

"After Anton Fox?"

"No, after St. Anton where the baby was conceived. We were there in April."

"What were you doing there?"

"Apart from the obvious?"

I flushed with embarrassment; Jo could not be embarrassed.

"A long way to go to conceive," I managed to say, then regretted it; maybe she was at some clinic for mental or physical problems.

"Some people will go to any lengths but we were ski-ing, it's George's latest passion."

"You two are a couple of dynamos, aren't you? Fast cars, flying, horse racing, and now ski-ing," I noted.

I was feeling more than a modicum of jealousy not about the ski-ing or horse racing but definitely the flying and driving. I had only been in a plane once and that was flying from one airfield to another. As for the cars, I was a petrol-head through and through; we called them motoring enthusiasts in those days. I had ordered a Mini as soon as they were launched in August 1959, three months before I had met Jo. I was a bit cramped inside but it was nippy and easy to park.

"Work hard and play hard," she bragged, flicking ash from her cigarette.

"Fight hard, too by the sound of things," I added, reminding her of her description of her struggle with the man in black.

"Yes, I learnt to fight from the *Quiet Man*," she joked.

Jo reminded me of a blonde version of Maureen O'Hara, full mouth, generous lips a straight long nose and a high brow, but Jo's hair was a lot longer, it reached down her back, and it was blonder.

"Well you didn't fight fair, like him," I complained.

"I was fighting for my life," she protested.

I think she felt guilty about fighting but she had no choice; it was her life in danger, literally.

"Not in line with the *Hippocratic Oath* kicking someone below the belt and leaving him with a burnt hand, is it?" I accused, smiling to show I was teasing.

We had been through many awful and gruelling experiences together so I was entitled.

"I had to guarantee my getaway, George called an ambulance and the police on my instructions, remember, you were not there, were you?" she remonstrated.

"Okay, I'll do the fighting next time, or Sergeant Stephens will."

"Well, I think our roles are flexible, it was me who found out about the crime ring in the first place and it was George who tracked us down when we were in trouble."

"I suppose you're right," I admitted, it was never easy to argue with Jo, she was used to getting her own way and beside all that, she was generally right.

"How is Sergeant Stephens?"

"Terry? He's well, fully recovered."

"Still a dab hand with a revolver?"

"Does Jo Murphy smoke too many *Senior Service* cigarettes?"

We both laughed uproariously. It was good to be in her company again. She was such great fun.

Maybe it's best if I start at the beginning of this caper. I know it was a long time ago but the story is worth telling, the world I lived in has changed for the better in so many ways but still, almost sixty years later some things have remained stubbornly the same. Women are still not valued adequately. People like Jo are never celebrated properly and the fairer sex is not appreciated or respected enough. It was ever thus.

- ii - Josephine

Nora Josephine Murphy was born in the pub where Dick Turpin famously shot his partner in crime.

The stables behind the Old Red Lion on Whitechapel High Street, now part of the East End was where the local constables grabbed Turpin's accomplice; Turpin decided to shoot one of them with his pistol, he had one shot to free his friend, Mathew King. There was a tremendous crack and the pistol smoked. The ball lodged in his associate's heart and King died instantly. Running through the back door and into the inn, Turpin threw himself through the front window and escaped. That had been in May 1737 and two years later, he was caught and executed in York.

Since then, the pub had grown and the street had spread on either side, running up to Mile End Gate to the East and Aldgate to the West. Opposite, a hospital was built in 1757.

The Royal London Hospital was across the road but Nora was born in one of the rooms above the pub, as there were no maternity wards there in 1922. Her birth on the 14th July, Bastille Day, was recorded at 94 Lever Street, London E1. Born within the sound of Bow Bells, she automatically became a cockney.

Her father, John Rickard Murphy, 'J.R.' to his friends, had been in the Royal Irish Constabulary'. The Old Red Lion in Whitechapel was his first pub. He had received his pension as a lump sum, stayed with his sister at the Three Cross Keys in *The City* and worked his way up to manager at *The Falcon* in Clapham Junction.

His wife, Catherine Conlon, or *Kitty* had four children, John, Michael, Moira and Nora; they were all healthy and tall like their father. *Kitty* and *JR* had a thriving pub and they were very close friends with local celebrity, Maurice Bloom, whose *kosher* restaurant was around the corner in Brick Lane. The tailors who worked nearby locked up their workshops and popped into *Murphy's* for a double scotch on the way home for their evening meal.

"Double Gold," was a constant cry in the pub.

A double gold, was a double scotch, gold watch is cockney rhyming slang for a scotch.

Kitty, the dutiful wife, flirted with the customers, provided them with gefilte fish and pickled herrings and looked after her children while John looked after the stock and kept an eagle eye on all staff, making sure they did not take too much from the till and protecting his cut of the profits as proprietor. He paid his staff well but he was a martinet, he expected everything to be shipshape in his hostelry, he checked the tops of doors for dust and mirrors and glasses for smears.

After thirty-seven different moves, Jo was evacuated to a new home, Bromley House, Kilpedder that J.R. had bought at the outbreak of war. It had belonged to the Duke of Wellington's family; one of the sons had died in the garages experimenting with engines. Her siblings were packed off to boarding school near Dublin.

Jo lived there throughout the war with *Kitty*. Every night she slept in a different one of the twelve bedrooms to keep the beds aired and she played billiards every day on her own in the billiard room until she could clear the table efficiently.

There was school but she frequently missed the bus into Dublin and when she did catch the bus she played truant and want to the cinema where Joseph Locke played the organ and sang.

After the war, they moved Rockmount in Dublin so Jo could attend the Royal Colleges of Surgeons while John Rickard Murphy worked in London building a business buying, turning around and selling pubs.

It was long hours and hard work but in the end there were sufficient rewards in the hard graft.

JR bought a big house in the suburbs, he made sure he had a cook and a driver who lived in and a cleaner who visited twice a week. Good food and fine wine were part and parcel of their life at weekends. When war had broke out JR had bought whiskey in bond, which made him some money and the bombs and road widening schemes had allowed him to sell pubs at a good price.

The docklands pubs were busy; it was where the dockers traded their purloined goods, the Irish workmen were moving into the East End and hankered after a good pint of Guinness as they built the new roads and houses after the war.

- iii - George

George Patrick Joseph Fitzpatrick was born, on 21st July 1921, in a Glebe; the birth certificate recorded the event as happening at The Neale nearby, not in the first floor room at Mile Hill House so he might have been born prematurely like his brother.

The parsonage of some fifty acres was built during the Napoleonic period in 1813; it was located between Lough Corrib and Lough Mask, in County Mayo. It was the parochial house of the grey stone Church of Ireland, edifice half way between Mile Hill and The Neale.

George's father, Patrick Fitzpatrick, was also a sergeant in the R.I.C., just like Mr. Murphy but he had been in a three man patrol in Cork city. The *Irish Republican Army* drove by in a car, shooting his two colleagues. The shock of seeing his two friends, on either side, being gunned down haunted him until his dying day.

Marrying Catherine Melotte, he settled in Mayo. The Civil War in The Irish Free State led to the founding of the Republic. Catherine's father had been a wool merchant and had bought up supplies of local wool before the outbreak of the First World War.

The price of raw wool rocketed with both sides needing blankets and uniforms, Patrick's father-in-law made a fortune and, with the proceeds, bought the Glebe from the English as they sold off their properties cheaply to the local population.

Patrick and Catherine had two children, Henry and George. Like Nora, George was the youngest; he was the most handsome of the family. She was the prettiest in hers. George was born big and bumptious, his brother Henry had weak eyesight and had been born prematurely so he was frail. Patrick read the newspapers, recovering from his experience, the shooting had affected him greatly, he had known his colleagues well and he often wondered why he had been spared the bullet. Contemplation and piano playing filled his days.

He was grateful for his good fortune.

The Glebe was a wonderful dowry and provided a good income. Catherine Melotte, another *Kitty*, rented the fields, drew water from the well in the stable yard, washed, tended the chickens, pigs and peacocks, cooked and cleaned, wearing herself out in the process.

She was a good wife, a loving aunt, daughter, mother and sister but more than that she worked tirelessly to balance the books, bring in an income from the farm and to look after her three boys.

Inevitably, she died young leaving Patrick and Henry to look after themselves while George went to the *Royal College of Surgeons* in Dublin and then on to London to carve his career in England.

The big draughty house built into the side of a hill was damp and cold but there were trees to provide wood for the fires, peat aplenty from the *Atlantic Blanket Bogs* of Donegal, Mayo, Galway, Kerry, Clare and Sligo and there was coal to be had from Ballingarry mines in Tipperary.

The *Royal Irish Constabulary*, though disbanded, had provided a generous pension. Combined with the income from The Glebe, the family lived well if not as well as the Murphy family across the water.

Chapter Three – Cedars Road

"Battersea, 7990," Jo announced into the Bakelite receiver, she twiddled her finger around the brown cord cable.

"Doctor Murphy?" I asked; my voice was hard and dry like gravel, I was tired and so were my men.

"Speaking," she replied putting on her best telephone manner but there was caution in her voice; this was obviously not a social call.

"I am sorry to disturb you on a Sunday night but I understand you are the duty pathologist, on-call today," I stammered.

"Yes, of course, you're right, and you are?"

"Detective Inspector Regan, Richard Regan, I am afraid we'll need your services tonight."

"Of course, Inspector, can you give me the address, please?" she asked, picking up a pencil and a sheaves of A5 paper piled neatly next to the telephone, *Fitzpatrick Brothers, Haymarket London SW1*, was written in embossed navy blue print on the top of each sheet. Her husband had branched out into owning pubs just like his father-in-law.

"Flat 5, Thornton Place, 48-52 Clapham Common North Side. It's at the top of Cedars Road."

"Thank you Inspector, I know it," she asserted.

"Really?" I replied, surprised.

"I live on the West Side. I can be there in fifteen minutes."

"Good, my men would appreciate that."

"I'll be there as soon as I can," she promised, "goodbye Inspector Regan."

"I look forward to seeing you soon, goodbye," I added, knowing that my voice had not softened during the call.

I had to remain professional much as I hated to disturb anyone's Sunday night. I was a copper, I'd signed up to inhospitable places and ungodly hours. I was intrigued that the duty pathologist should be a woman. It piqued my interest, nothing more, I imagined a Miss Marple type, what I actually got was pure glamour.

Jo had hung up when she heard the click of disconnection.

Looking at black marble mantle clock, on the dining room, mahogany, mantle-piece she saw it was ten o'clock. George was not yet home, inspecting the pubs but the children were upstairs at the top of the house in bed in their rooms; Catherina and Georgina, were a year apart in age, the eldest, Catherina was seven years old, Georgina was six, both had been born in August; a day and a year apart.

Their Swiss nanny slept in the bedroom between them on the top floor. Their only boy Patrick was four and he was on the second floor, sleeping next to his parent's room, in the Blue Room, the nursery.

Jo's medical bag was out in the hallway; a standard lamp with a pale green shade guided her to the double doors at the front of the house.

A fire burnt in the grate, a copper guard encased an exquisite glossy green tiled Art Nouveau fireplace, a Moroccan design, surrounded by mahogany boxing. Flame danced around the coals. She warmed herself by the fire for a moment as she checked her bag, stethoscope, auriscope, blood-pressure kit and pathologist paraphernalia, including blank *Death Certificates*.

There was a spacious coat cupboard under the stairs opposite the fire from which she chose a green, three-quarter-length, wool coat. She turned the door handle and slipped into the night. Outside in Wakehurst Road her car stood under a lamppost, a Marlin and strato blue, two-tone, 1942. *Nash 600 Ambassador 6 Slipstream Sedan*; it was streamlined and sleek, a beautiful expression of modern design.

Her father had shipped it over from America for Jo to drive while she was at the *Royal College of Surgeons* in Dublin.

There was no alternative; car production in England had been halted by the war yet in America, the smaller car producers had continued production whilst their larger competitors produced trucks and tanks.

The leather seats were cold and the windows had condensation on them but she was wrapped up warm. Jo started the engine and the windscreen wipers came on with   a flick of a switch.

Wiping the inside of the glass cleared her enough space in the large windscreen to drive safely, the efficient heater was already clearing the condensation at the bottom. Once her view was clear, she drove left onto the West Side and filtered onto the South Circular Road, racing towards Battersea Rise, then turned right onto the A3 heading to Clapham Old Town.

Within ten minutes, Jo had parked the car and was introducing herself to the policeman posted outside the entrance on Cedars Road. "Good evening Constable," she sighed breathlessly.

"Good evening, you must be the pathologist."

"Yes, Doctor Murphy, we're the only people out and about at this ungodly hour."

"First floor, Doctor."

"Thank you officer."

He informed the Inspector of her arrival through the intercom at the top of the steps and opened the door for her. She bounded up the stairs remembering the races she used to have with the other students to the *Rotunda* to deliver a baby.

The first one to reach the round delivery room always delivered the baby; the runners up had to wait around the hospital until they had a delivery. A dozen deliveries had to be made before qualification in midwifery; a dozen times she ensured she reached the delivery room, first. The *Rotunda* was the first *lying-in-hospital* in the world but the doctors did most of the lying around. Jo had wanted to go to bed not hang around a hospital dayroom in the middle of Dublin waiting to deliver a baby so she ran faster.

I stood in the open doorway, wearing my brown trilby and a beige trench coat as well as a hangdog expression; the truth was I needed sleep and had not got it; my first baby, Alec, was teething and I was working longer and longer hours without a break. When I was younger, I was considered a handsome man and Jo was beautiful. We smiled at each other, an acknowledgment of our prowess, and a salute to our sacrifice in public service and to show we had good teeth.

I think one or other of the two policemen in the flat noticed a slight frisson between us but we all shrugged it off. I took off my hat, holding it in my left hand so I could shake hands with her.

She had a firm grip; I was impressed. I spoke first, welcoming her; I was beholden to do so.

"Good Evening, again, Doctor, thank you for coming so quickly, I'm impressed you made it here so quickly, normally fifteen minutes is an hour in medical circles."

I had spent long evenings waiting for doctors to finish their meals.

"Good evening; I suppose you could say it was fortunate that I was so close," she replied, ignoring his barbed comment about her fellow physicians.

"Let me introduce you to P.C. Watkins and Sergeant Stephens, they responded to the call and contacted me, just in case," I explained.

"Good evening Gentlemen," she said smiling at both men, they returned her greeting with slight nods and small smiles, "What have we got Inspector Regan?"

"Suicide, from what I can gather, a gas fire left on, we've opened the windows," I explained, moving to one side to let her proceed gesturing with a flamboyant arc of my arm that the room was hers.

"Thank you inspector," she responded, taking in the scene.

The flat was sparsely decorated, a sofa, a low table and a *Garrad* Radiogram. I nodded towards it.

"Ray Charles on the turntable and *The BBC World Service* on the radio, it was switched on when we arrived, the radio was on quite loudly. His name was Stephen Allen."

"The suicide note?" she asked.

"Not as far as I can see, my men have searched the flat," I assured her looking deep into those beautiful blue eyes.

She held my gaze.

"Interesting."

What was interesting; the information or me? I was not sure and then she looked away, looking at the body curled up on the floor.

"Psychology is your field, too?" I asked.

"A little," she admitted, "we all do a some psychology at medical school; it's and interest."

"Really," I said dryly, it sounded   sarcastic but she did not flinch.

"It's just strange," she noted.

"In my experience, there is no pattern to this crime," I insisted.

"Crime?"

"Isn't it a crime to take a life, either yours or someone else's?" I answered acidly.

"You're right," agreed Jo, she had signed the *Hippocratic oath*; she viewed me in a new light.

She told me later, she felt I was less of a hard-bitten detective and clearly a philosopher as well as an investigator.

We walked towards the body and stopped, standing over him. The corpse was lying close to the gas fire, slumped on the carpet; his left hand showed the fissures of his palm, it seemed to be reaching out for the fireplace, his curled fingers reaching out for the source of his demise.

His right arm lay across his chest. His face seemed serene. His body was curled up as if he were trying to snuggle up in bed. He had been wearing grey flannel trousers, a brown belt and a white cotton shirt covered by a burgundy cardigan.

His shoes were off and his black wool socks had been darned on the right big toe. Jo put her medical bag on the table behind the sofa and walking around the furniture, she bent to examine the dead man before speaking.

"Well, I would say he looks very healthy, his cheeks are rosy, the classic sign of gas poisoning. A blood test will confirm the amount of carboxyhaemoglobin in the blood," she said.

"Yes, Doctor, the autopsy will give us most of what we need to proceed, you've confirmed my suspicions."

"Good, I'll examine the body and, then, we'll do the paperwork," she announced.

"I appreciate your thoroughness."

I did but I also wanted to get home to bed in Trott Street with my wife and baby sleeping next to me.

As Jo crouched to examine the body, she took hold of his right hand, it was cold and it had no pulse. The coolness of a dead body always filled her with dread.

She knew beyond doubt that he was dead but she still went through the procedures. It was a routine, almost a ritual but it calmed her down and helped her to both detached and methodical at the same time.

She had been trained to an extremely high standard and she would leave nothing to chance: 'check and double check'; that had been drilled into her; only a thorough examination would yield certainty.

All avenues had to be explored. After a thorough examination, she was satisfied with her prognosis. The inspector shifted uncomfortably on one leg, he had not expected her to take so long and he was relieved to find she was finally finished.

"How long have you been here, Inspector?" she asked.

"The incident was reported at seven fifteen, he was meant to meet a friend for supper, the friend phoned us and the occupant in number six smelt gas, so a beat bobby called it in about eight. We're at Lavender Hill so we were around here pretty sharpish. Otherwise he could have been here for days," I explained.

"That would not have been ideal for any of us, I'm glad you were able to act so quickly," she noted drily.

Jo examined the body, probing with her fingers, examining the eyelids, the nose, the mouth and the skin on his arms. She turned his head and moved it from side to side before gently laying it down on the carpet again. She returned to her case on the table.

What do you think doctor?" I asked.

"Well, I would say he died between two and three hours ago," she asserted.

"Really, how so, Doctor?" I was a young copper and dead bodies were not a currency I was familiar with, I was fascinated by the fact that doctors could work out the rough time of death and I wanted to know how they knew.

"Primary flaccidity is still there, *rigor mortis* is just setting into the eyelids but it has not advanced to the mouth or the neck."

"Keep going, I'll let you know when you've lost me," I fixed my eyes on her to show I meant it. My men could tolerate a few more minutes.

"Obviously, the mortuary will give a more accurate time. They'll measure glycogen levels among other things. We'll have a much clearer idea of the exact time of   death once they have finished."

Efficiently, she packed her medical bag again while talking. She was aware that my men and I were keen to get back to the station, file our reports and finish our shift without further incident.

"Right, we'll leave that to the *boffins* at the *morgue*," I decided, we had been hanging around here for a long time.

It was time to leave.

"One other factor is the ambient temperature," Jo continued, "when conditions are warm, the onset and pace of rigor mortis are sped up, providing an ideal environment for the metabolic processes that cause decay."

"Go on," I urged.

"It's very warm in here so I would have expected him to be further along the process," she noted.

I acknowledged her point by raising a quizzical eyebrow; I suspected there was more than just the time of death on her mind.

"Yes, the building is warm, some form of central boiler system feeding radiators in all the flats providing background heating; there's hardly any need for fires according to the caretaker, we have not been idle since we arrived. You're saying he might have died at a later hour than we thought"

"It's likely, but there's one other thing I noticed, Inspector?"

"Really what's that?" I asked.

"A bruising around the neck," she said.

"Go on, I'm listening intently," I assured her.

"There is chance that some sort of struggle preceded the poisoning."

"You mean there's a possibility it wasn't suicide after all."

"Only, a possibility, the pathologist at the morgue will know more, of course. An examination would reveal any blows to the head and a more detailed look at the neck may yield the answers. Just ask the pathologist to look out for signs that this was not suicide. They are generally very good at spotting inconsistencies."

"Not necessarily, junior pathologists sometimes miss details," I informed her and clearly by implication so do police officers. Both Sergeant Stephens and I had examined the body for any signs of foul play and we had both concluded that any injuries were due to the fall. We did not see any reason to suspect anything but suicide.

That was what they had wanted of course.

"You have a point," she admitted readily, she smiled; Nora liked his no nonsense approach.

"Everyone, makes mistakes; to me it looked like a straightforward suicide," I explained, "the position of the body, the tap on the gas fire turned on. That's why the windows were open. Even we missed the evidence that you spotted."

I was candid and philosophical, which was a change for me but I felt immediately that I could trust this beautiful, tall, elegant woman with my life.

"That's because you were waiting for me to do the examination and you did not want to disturb the body," she assured me, "I cannot see any obvious contusions to the cranium but I can feel a few bumps and lumps on the skull. I would say this man fought before dying; there are traces of blood under his fingernails. They look like dirt but I have swabbed them and it looks like blood. A more thorough examination will show whether this is from an assailant or form his scratching an old cut."

"In that case, I'll see you after the autopsy at the morgue tomorrow at ten," I insisted.

Jo was about to argue but a stern look from me silenced her. My brown eyes bored into her and made all protestation useless. She could go willingly or she could be forced to go. The former was preferable. We knew, even then, that our paths might cross again.

"Of course, Inspector, I'll complete the death certificate as far as I am able, you and your men can be on your way. I should be able to move some appointments from my morning surgery to the afternoon. It will take some juggling in the waiting room but I can manage, I think."

"Thank you, that would be helpful. We've found his driving licence you can copy the details from there," I explained, handing over the document.

"That's perfect, thank you."

"So you think there could have been a murder in Cedars Road?" I asked incredulously, it seemed like a simple suicide to me.

"There is evidence for that," she said seriously. "I would say it is likely there has been a Murder on Cedar's Road."

"Thank you for your prognosis," I responded, we smiled at our use of each other's terminology. Jo picked up on the joke and smiled back. She dared to quote the Bard and see my response.

"Who worse than a physician, would this report become?" she announced.

"These are troubled times, scarce a day goes by when a king does not lose his crown," I replied, reddening at his poor knowledge of Shakespeare; it was the only quote I knew, it was my father's favourite quote.

"Trouble comes not in single spies but in battalions," Jo added, handing over the certificate and bowing.

"Thank you doctor," I said, taking the certificate, "Until tomorrow?"

"Until tomorrow, goodbye" she answered, "Tomorrow and tomorrow, and tomorrow, creeps in this petty pace from day to day."

As she spoke she swept from the room. All three officers looked at each other but kept their thoughts to themselves. It was no ordinary day, it was no ordinary suicide and she was no ordinary pathologist.

Chapter Four – The Autopsy and Normality

i

I was disturbed to know about a murder in 'My Manor'; Jo told me she was worried about the fact that a murder had been committed less than a ten-minute-walk from her home. We were both unsettled when we met in Falcon Road. Sergeant Stephens dropped me off before driving on to investigate a burglary in Battersea Park Road.

The Coroner's Office on Falcon Road was near Clapham Junction Station. It was an old-fashioned working class community with two up and two down houses, which had been deemed slums and were going to be cleared. They did not look too bad to me. The windows were clean and when I arrived ten minutes before eight, I saw a teenage girl being sent out to scrub the steps; the windows on most of the properties were clean.

The area was proud and poor, not dingy and dirty. From my time on the beat, I knew people were generally happy there. There were no gardens but these people worked so hard and travelled so far to work that they had no time for gardening; they washed in their sculleries using boiled water from the kettle and a tin basin and the toilet was outside.

It was a community that looked after and cared about each other; there were some rogues but we knew who they were, the others greeted their neighbours and sent to the pub for a jug of beer each night to help with the drudgery of ironing and polishing shoes. That was the first thing Jo noticed that morning, I take pride in my shoes, a habit instilled in me by my father; you could see your face in mine. My Dad was a copper; I wanted to be like him. Jo had commented on my shoes. I get them from an outfit in Brick Lane, good quality Northamptonshire shoes, leather up and leather soled. You cannot beat a well-made English shoe in my humble opinion.

Outside, I stood admiring the colour and curves of her *Nash*. I love four things, women, cigarettes and alcohol, not necessarily in that order and above all cars, the shape, the size and the smell of leather.

A woman is a woman, fascinating and awe-inspiring Cigarettes are perfect cylinders of pleasure and cars are the epitome of man's ingenuity. The American motorcar was a real beauty as shiny as my shoes and of similar quality. The roof was light blue like a stratus sky and the bodywork was the colour of a marlin fish, that deep rich, dark, deep blue of a fathomless ocean, it looked incongruous under the grey curtain of cloud, the white wall tyres, the sleek lines, all at sea in the wilderness of two-up-two-down Victorian houses built for the railway workers.

"So what do you think, doctor?" I asked, tearing my eyes away from the beautiful mass of metal. It was not difficult Jo's eyes were twice as magnetic. I could have stared into them all day and her body was more beautiful, too.

"I think we should have a cigarette," she replied, "would you care for one of mine?"

"*Senior Service*? Yes please," I replied gratefully, an expensive cigarette was a treat.

I smoked *Wild Woodbine*; if it was good enough for the men in the trenches, it was good enough for me. It was a pleasant tobacco; I smoked the filter-tipped ones, which made them less strong. Having a non-filter was 'bliss' as Jo would say.

"Pleasure," she intoned, pushing the box from below to reveal the white sticks of tobacco. I helped myself; she lit my cigarette with her gas lighter before I could rummage in my raincoat for my petrol lighter.

"Thank you for showing me what you found, it means that this is more of a murder enquiry than a simple suicide, " I observed, to fill the silence, two addicts indulging in their tobacco fixation. I had read a bit of Freud when I was at Hendon.

"I'm just glad the coroner corroborated my prognosis, it's important to make sure in cases like this," she responded, drawing smoke into her lungs.

"We, now, know for sure the murderer was left handed or at least used his left hand to commit the   murder," I asserted.

"That should narrow things down, once you find the person responsible," she added, it did not sound like she held out much hope of finding the killer.

"You've been very thorough, this vital evidence could easily have been missed," I assured her, exhaling slowly and smiling. "I'm grateful."

"So what happens, now?" Jo asked, she had folded her arms, her right hand holding her cigarette close to her generous mouth, held between her index and middle finger.

"The case will be investigated by the New Scotland Yard," I explained. "They had their fingerprint people at the flat first thing, they'll look for treads on the floor from unfamiliar shoes. We ensured the flat was disturbed as little as possible. I am sure they will let me know their findings in due course.

"So, you won't be involved?" she gasped.

"I'm afraid it's no longer in my hands, " I answered, trying not to show how disappointed I was.

"But you found the body, won't you be involved in the investigation?" she asked, sounding as if she felt it was unfair.

"No, I'm based at Battersea, it's no longer my case. CID will handle the case; they'll use my report to establish their premise and work from there. Don't worry, I know the investigating officer, I'm sure they'll keep me informed and if they do, I'll let you know. Most murder cases are easy to solve. It's generally someone the victim knows, there are few unpremeditated murders in this day and age."

"That's reassuring," she said, I could almost taste the irony in the wind.

"The Criminal Investigation Department are at the flat, now. They'll deal with the details; you'll read about it in the Evening paper. However, if you want to talk about the case you'll find me at Lavender Hill," I continued, rules were rules. She was married and I was married, the case would be solved and we would most probably never see each other again. That's what I felt at the time.

We were kindred spirits, both good-looking, we shared the confederacy of good-looking people, we had both had our share of unwanted advances; it was the curse of being pleasing to look at.

As much as we appreciated our mutual situation, we understood the conventions of the time, marriage was sacred; she was married and I was married, we would never cheat on our spouses. There were codes and rules for everyone in those days and for the sake of society we followed them. That was one, maybe the only good thing about that time. You knew where you stood and understood the rules were for everyone, of course there were exceptions, cads and criminals. We avoided them.

"If I do think of something, can I rely on you to take it to the other investigators?" she asked cryptically.

"It's my duty to help the *C.I.D.* in any way that I can, of course you can. I owe you a favour; you helped us detect a murder where we would have dismissed the incident as suicide. We'll keep you abreast of developments, never you fear."

"Thank you Inspector, I appreciate it."

"I have to thank you, we'll look more carefully before we jump to conclusions, my officers and I, but that's off the record," I conceded.

"Strictly off the record," she laughed, unlocking the car door.

"I look forward to working together again and thanks for the cigarette."

"Pleasure, if there's nothing else inspector? I have a waiting room full of patients."

"You've been most helpful, let me get the door for you," I offered, opening the door for her.

"Thank you."

She slipped into her seat and I closed the door gently behind her, doffing my trilby in salute. We smiled at each other as kindred spirits, we were both attracted to each other and perhaps if we had met much earlier in our lives, we may have at least become sweethearts, might even have married but life was not about 'ifs'; it was about getting on and doing the job. I liked her, I fancied her, too, and I wanted to think that she reciprocated the feelings, but even if she had, there was nothing either of us would do. It's different, now, then, there was a code of conduct to adhere to, now, people do as they fancy. It seems all too casual to me. Friendship was all we had to offer each other and in the weeks to come we would need all the friends we could get.

Jo went back to her routine, if you could call it such. Her days were more varied than mine. I had to liaise with the other detectives, write up reports and carry on with my job plus look after the misses and the nipper. It was exhausting.

Jo's surgery opened early, Mrs. Haines had scrubbed the two steps up to the doorway on Wakehurst Road. The hedge to the left had been kept trimmed by a man who cut back the foliage all along the common and the white paint stripe that ran across the wall at waist height had been newly painted.

Mrs. Haines had polished the stained glass window on the first landing inside and out; using a small stepladder to get to the street side of the window. The art nouveau lead and glass took an age to clean but with her care and labour the glass gleamed like new and the lead seemed blacker and more solid.

George had already left to prepare for his Harley Street clinics, at his Uncle Henry's practice at number 186. He had taken it over when Henry had retired. Jo had wanted to be a vet and had been persuaded that humans would benefit more from her contribution to medical science.

George had wanted to be a specialist ever since his uncle had arrived at the Glebe in his Rolls Royce Silver Ghost. From that day, he was determined to become a doctor as it would make him a wealthy man. It had of course. Both Jo and he had worked hard at medical college and afterwards, their motivation was different; she was to heal the sick, he wanted to do better than her father, in a shorter time and with less business acumen. Jo opened the surgery at seven thirty and the receptionist led a procession of patients into the hall with the wooden fireplace and the Moroccan green tiles reminiscent of the great pre-Raphaelite, Lord Leighton and his house near Holland Park. They were encouraged to wipe their feet before treading on the Persian rug that had been laid to protect the parquet floor.

They were able to check themselves in the long hall mirror opposite the door where Jo religiously brushed her hair each morning. There were four doors, one immediately to the left, the study and that was the waiting room, two doors dead ahead, the door to the left was the surgery, the drawing room on the bell system and to the right the dining room, the fourth door on the far right led into the kitchen. They were all pine, stained such a deep mahogany to be appear almost black, however, their brass plates and Mexican hat doorknobs had been diligently polished by Mrs Haines.

The receptionist, Bubs Kirmode, would call seat them on some old pub chairs that had green cushions on the seat and take the first patient in, knocking on the door before opening it and announcing the patient's name, before closing the door. Bubs would keep the fire going in the small hearth in the corner of the room. The study had two sash windows that looked out onto the front garden, a baby grand in one corner and the seating in an L shape in the other. Her desk was next to the door, opposite the windows and beside the fire.

The reception door was always kept open so she could hear the patient closing the door as they left. Some went straight out into the street in a hurry, some came in to say thank you before they left. Most days, Bubs would, listen for the patient to come out, take the new one in and lead the previous patient to the door allowing them to talk about the next steps if they so wished. I remember Jo telling me years later about her surgery and its efficient yet relaxed atmosphere. I saw the surgery once. You walked into the room and it was amazing.

There was a huge free standing set of book shelves on the wall to the right of the door, it was the first thing you noticed, five tiers high and reaching the dido rail. It was over seven foot tall and must have been twelve foot wide. It was filled with medical books old exercise books that looked like they were bound by Victorians, all dark leather and vellum paper.

The textbooks were all hard back, too and medical journals had wine red covers. The next thing you noticed was the mantelpiece. It was stunning, looking like a Nash original; the builder of the house had been a successful developer in the area and had spared no expense in design and materials. The wooden mantel was painted white; it had a circular mirror in the centre and a triptych design, the leaves being Nash style urns complete with beads surrounding them.

The house was a tasteful nod to previous styles; each room had a particular theme and feel. The hearth had been surrounded by the most exquisite orange, almost pink marble and there were wooden columns and dados running up the sides. I love beautiful things. In the grate, a fire burnt to take the chill off the morning, the coals glowing satisfyingly thanks to Mrs Haines. Moisture had already started to settle on the windowpanes demonstrating how cold it was outside.

The wallpaper complimented the room, it was a classical pattern with green throughout a real regency effect, which would have been more at home in a Georgian house than an Edwardian one but there it worked.

Opposite the fireplace on one of the longer walls was a servant's bell, which allowed her to summon Mr Haines who would bring some more hot water for Jo to wash her hands with between patients. Underneath this was a Victorian glass cabinet with some *Scott's Emulsion and Pulmo Bailly* for coughs, *Aspirin* and *Alka Seltzer* on the bottom glass shelf. There was magnesium sulphate paste, merbromin, iodine, plasters, antiseptic cream, bandages and white spirit on the top shelf.

Jo's desk was in the recess of the large bay windows; the main one looked east, the one to the left looked to the Northside of the common and the one to the right to the Southside. Behind the desk was Jo's chair and in front were two chairs from one of her father's pub, bentwood but with a green cushion on the seat. Often husbands and wives would come as a couple to consultations.

On the desk were two piles of the patients' notes by Jo's right arm. On the far side sat a white marble cigarette box, a green onyx table lighter and an elegant green stone ashtray. No one could be in any doubt that Jo's favourite colour was green.

She would not be behind the desk when you went in, she would be striding across the room to greet you with a warm, firm handshake. Then, she would offer you a chair and once you were seated, she would offer you a cigarette. It was through making her patients feel valued that she gained her reputation

Everything was designed to put the patient at their ease. A patient who feels relaxed is far more likely to confide in their physician. That was the idea and it worked, she had a fabulous reputation as a thorough and caring doctor. I know, I checked locally, Sergeant Stephens also backed up my research by making his own enquiries. She came out with glowing references.

One time she told me later, she had a syphilitic patient who claimed he had contracted the disease from a toilet seat. Syphilis can only be contracted in one way.

Jo coolly offered him a cigarette and when he accepted it and lit it, she said, "You'll have to tell me the name of that toilet seat, we caught you before you infected anyone else, we have to make sure that said seat does not infect anyone."

"Of course, you're right doctor," he conceded and gave her the name of the woman.

Everyone who came to the surgery received the utmost care and attention, a thorough examination and a sympathetic ear. Sometimes couples could not get their babies to sleep. Jo sympathised, Georgina her second born had also hardly slept so much so that Jo had gone to see Martin Walsh the other GP in the area to ask for advice.

On other occasions people came to the surgery just to talk; they would smoke a cigarette and discuss bereavement, or their tiredness or their boredom at the drudgery of life. They discussed personal problems and they asked for advice, she presented the options. She was as much a psychologist as a medical practitioner. She healed the body and the mind.

She was still on the General Practitioners rota for duty pathologist at weekends, but that was to be the extent of her involvement in police matters. Every six weeks she was on call at weekends to attend any incidents that needed a pathologist present. There was no reason for us to see each other and we returned to our normal lives. Mine was keeping crime off the streets hers was healing her patients. It was a time when public service was respected much more.

So what about me at this time; was I pining over Jo, hoping to see her. I was married and very much in love with my wife, Susie and my baby boy Bartholomew. We had bought a two bedroom, garden flat that formed part of an old Victorian house at the top end of Maple Road in Penge and coincidently Jo's father owned the *London Tavern* at one end of the street. I could not get away from her but I was busy with so many cases, my head was spinning.

There was a lot more crime than everyone thinks in those days and a fair few fights in pubs every night, after all in those days they were packed. We also had more than our fair share of domestic violence.

If you went to the Falcon on a Friday or Saturday night, there was bound to be a fight. Broken bottles, smashed glasses, table and chairs would be involved just like a fight at a saloon bar in a 'Western'. A lot of the time it was a domestic argument between a man and a woman that would spark it off. They'd get in first, she smashing his half-pint brown bottle for his 'light and bitter', he smashing the top off her cut glass 'port and lemon' sherry copita.

Battersea and Clapham were working class areas. Burglary was rife, people did keep their back doors unlocked but only because they had nothing to nick or a relative was looking after the baby. We lived in Maple Road because Susie's mother and grandmother lived on the street.

You might have whole families, three our four generations, uncles and aunts living in the streets around south London and the East End. North and west London was more fluid. Battersea was no exception, and if they were a family of villains, they kept up the family tradition. We knew who they all were but that did not mean we could always catch them and catching them in the act was the only way we would get a conviction. Still, we knew who they were, who to ask and who to search and whose lock-up to rummage through.

Car theft was a huge problem as well. There were no steering column locks and cars were easily hot-wired, *National Service* had ensured there were lots of lorry drivers but also lots of mechanics and they were able to pass on the technique. The locks on the cars were generally easy to pick if you had a good set of tools and knew what you were doing.

Every day there was another list of crimes to investigate and hopefully solve. It took a lot of footwork and perseverance but above all it all took time. I hardly saw Susie and the baby with the workload and Sergeant Stephens complained that he never had enough time to play football with his two sons, Ben and Tim.

Chapter Five – Breakfast and Bacon - Venus, the Bringer of Peace

There was a thump as a package landed on the tiled floor beyond the inner door. Sunlight had briefly permeated the gap between the inner and outer doorways. It was the letterbox opening and closing. Jo was in the hall brushing her long locks in the mirror, she had backcombed leaning forward and had stood up straight to brush out the hair so it fell away from her face.

Her eye had seen the flash of light; she had heard the sound of the package landing on the floor. That made sense, light travelled faster than sound, it was nothing to worry about.

She had been concerned about the murder and her nerves were on edge, she could smell danger in the air, she and Regan were investigating a murder, her female intuition was something she listened out for, it told her she was in peril and it had not failed her so far.

Placing her comb into the bristles of her long-handled brush, she left her grooming kit on the ledge of the fireplace, the wooden one in the hall, with the Moorish tiling that seemed to proffer a tribute to Lord Leighton and his house in Kensington.

Striding over to the cream-coloured front door and turning the small brass handle, there was a reassuring click and the door opened smoothly after that. Pulling the door fully open to the right, she looked at the package on the floor. It lay in front of the double-doors that led out into Wakehurst Road.

Swiftly, she bent at the knees to pick up the brown paper parcel; it was rectangular. It was heavy but she suspected what it was.

The handwriting and postmark were familiar. Picking up the rectangular package, she closed the door and walked through the hall. There were four doors leading off the hall, she chose the one on the far right. George was upstairs, he   had just returned from his clinics.

The routine was for him to hang up his suit jacket, have a quick wash, change his shirt and then have his lunch.

He had attended a private eye clinic on Harley Street at eight to nine thirty, followed by another clinic at St. George's Hospital at Hyde Park Corner from ten to twelve thirty.

There was still rationing so the midday repast was not a sumptuous meal, it may have caused him to fall asleep in his afternoon clinics if it had been, he worked very long hours and was not immune to the soporific affects of serotonin.

After his lunch, he would go on to St. George's Hospital near Tooting Broadway for the eye clinic from two to five. Then, he would bathe in the huge cast iron bath and visit his burgeoning pub business.

Returning to the hall and closing the front door, she hurried towards the right and the last of four brown doors that led from the hall, she turned the palm-sized brass oval knob, there was a tiny corridor, a dark brown stained door had to be pushed open, leading into a tiny hallway, then the kitchen door, painted cream, had to be pushed.

It had been designed to separate the kitchen area from the main house, trapping sounds and smells in its dark recesses. She found herself in a white tiled room and the heat from the *Aga* hit her as she stepped into the kitchen. The *Aga* was coal fired and emanated a constant heat that took the chill from most days. The kitchen was the only room that did not have condensation on the inside of the windows every morning.

The white rectangular tiles, arranged portrait style, stretched from skirting board to ceiling. Above the kitchen door was a brown panel with all the various rooms labelled to alert staff to where they were required. She walked through the large kitchen, dresser to the right, beyond which was the cellar door; the *Aga* was to the left. She passed the large window and dining table that had been pushed against the wall underneath. The door to the cellar was between the dresser and the kitchen window. It was painted in cream like the dresser.

Entering through the open door, she left behind the warmth of the kitchen and strode into cool scullery, the tiled floor replacing the red *Formica* floor of the kitchen, her high heels click-clacked like wheels on a railway track. The ceiling to skirting-board white tiles were square in the scullery. On the floor were red tiles about half the size of those on the wall. It was all designed to keep the area cool.

To her left was a huge American style double sink, a *Dainty Maid*, wood laminated and painted white, on top of which was a fully functioning American dishwasher that took up most of space on the draining board and a rectangular sash window, painted cream, overlooking the back garden.

To her right was a massive American *Kelvinator* fridge and ahead of her, slightly to the left, was a *Hotpoint* washing machine. She ignored all these fripperies of modern life. Instead, she pulled open the larder door to the right and walked into the cool room. The heavy black slate shelf felt cold to touch as her hand brushed the surface.

Opening the package, peeling back the wrapping paper, she revealed greaseproof paper around an almost rectangular object. Jo bent down, there was a wine rack underneath and on top of that were two heavy pans for use of the hob.

Selecting the one on the left, she placed it on the slate and straightened as she did so. The pan had a layer of lard at the bottom; it was beef dripping that had hardened when it cooled. Jo waited for the lard to heat into oil. Taking two rashers from inside the paper she placed them on the pan, folded the rest back into the package and left the dark larder, the cool scullery and returned to the warmth of the kitchen.

There was a box of eggs and a large white china plate waiting on the red *Formica* surface of the cream dresser. Using a bread knife, Jo sliced two pieces off a bloomer loaf and cutting off the crusts on the breadboard, she cut a square in the dough bread, which she put on the plate.

Moving the plate onto the *Aga* in the space between each hob to warm it, she casually placed the two squares and one piece of bread in the pan and fried them both on each side, popping them on the plate, she flipped the bacon and took the second slice and fried that on both sides. She flipped the bacon onto the plate. Taking both fried slices with the square holes she placed them in the piping hot beef dripping, cracking an egg into each hole. Just allowing enough time for the egg to fry slightly, she flipped the fried slices so the egg cooked on the other side.

The *egg-in-the-hole*, it should have been egg in the square space, was a deliciously rich breakfast treat that Jo had seen cooked in an American film. George adored the dish. It was especially delicious with two rashers of bacon from Bromley.

Within five minutes, there was a hot pan, cooling between the two hob covers and a plate with two rashers of bacon and two egg-in-the-holes sitting on the kitchen table. George looked at his *Longines 1948* watch, a gift from Jo so he would not be late for dates. It was precisely one o'clock; he had fifteen minutes to eat his lunch.

"Bacon?" he asked appreciatively, as he sat at the table.

"It arrived in the post ten minutes ago," she replied.

"From your mother in Wicklow?" he probed, cutting into the meat.

"She sent it from Kilpedder at five yesterday afternoon."

"The postal service is good."

"Not that good, it missed the morning post."

"Good enough, bacon is better for lunch when I am more awake."

"Enjoy it, it will give you strength."

Jo never ate the bacon that her mother sent from Ireland, she saved it all for George to eat. Meat was still rationed even though some goods were no longer under restriction but meat was still rare and expensive. Her mother sent it to her out of love and she gave every last rasher to George out of love.

"Remind me where are you off to at the weekend?" George asked.

"I'm going to visit Birmingham, this weekend" she replied, "Peg has offered to help me with this mystery on Cedar's Road."

"Astonishing, good luck to you both," he added before cutting into his egg and watching the yolk ooze over the bacon.

Chapter Six – A Ton to Birmingham - Mercury, the Winged Messenger

Jo eased the brown two-tone *Rolls* off the roundabout, onto the slip road and into the inside lane of the motorway.

George, ever- the-generous and thoughtful husband, had leant the car to her as he was flying to Le Touquet for a weekend of golf and he preferred their third car a large *Jaguar* when he was driving to Lydd Airport and he was flying with *Silver City Airways* which ran a car carrying air ferry using *Bristol Freighters*. Strangely enough, it was one of the busiest airports in England; a quarter of a million people used it each year. Needless to say I was not one of them.

The Swiss nanny was looking after the three children.

She loved the *Rolls*. The speed and luxury and the ease of driving made eating up the miles an absolute pleasure. The five litre six cylinder was as smooth as silk. The *Silver Cloud* was supremely comfortable, thick wool carpet, fat leather seats and walnut throughout, the smell, look and feel of opulence. White wall tyres gave it an American glamour.

The journey to Watford where the *M1* began, meant driving down Cedars Road, crossing Chelsea Bridge, negotiating Knightsbridge, passing Paddington, finding Finchley Road, brushing by Barnet and Bushy before finally reaching the new black top motorway, the first of its kind in England.

The first part of the *M1* had only opened on 2nd November 1959 by the Minister of Transport, Ernest Marples, only three weeks before; there was no central reservation, no crash barriers, no lighting and no speed limits.

Jo pressed her foot down, the *Rolls* cleaved through the early morning mist, hitting sixty, rather than easing off, she pressed on to seventy, settling down into a comfortable cruising speed, after a mile, less than a minute, she pushed the car on to eighty. After half a mile she was up to ninety and still she could not hear the engine. The brute power appealed to her.

As Watford became a speck in Jo's rear view mirror, she sped up to a hundred miles an hour. She cruised at that speed for as long as the motorway allowed. The road was clear except for a truck in the inside lane, Jo did not slow as she was in the outside lane.

All she could hear was the ticking of the clock.

There was no sound coming from the engine and only her swift progress reminded her of the fact she was driving and not sitting in a stationary car. George had bought the *Rolls* because it was a lot less conspicuous than a security van and could carry a ton of weight.

All the cash from his pubs, particularly *The Lord Rodney's Head*, could be transported in the boot of the car without a problem and without attracting attention to its cargo. Who would use a car as a security van?

Jo had no idea that this sedate saloon could be so much fun to drive. Sadly, the motorway was too short to really enjoy the experience for long, it petered out at Rugby. The rest of the journey was conducted at half the speed. She felt elated at having done one hundred miles an hour; she loved the idea that she could travel a mile in 36 seconds.

Jo was sufficiently aware of the vernacular to know about bikers doing a ton-up on that same motorway. It was in the press. Birmingham was 120 miles away so she could have done the journey in much less than the three and a half hours it actually took her.

Admittedly, a good hour was used getting across London. Although the motorway had been speedy, she was stuck behind various slow moving vehicles including a Messerschmitt KR200 three wheeler, bubble car, a tractor and a slow moving horsebox trailer attached to an ancient, 1948, *Land Rover*.

Arriving in Birmingham, she parked in Shadwell Street, outside St. Chad's Cathedral, the first Catholic Cathedral erected in the country since the Protestant Reformation. Completed in1841, it was designed by Pugin, who was also responsible for the Palaces of Westminster and the iconic clock tower of Big Ben. Jo was fond of his style of architecture and she even knew his first two names were Augustus Welby, she had read a book about him at *Bromley*, the house she stayed in during the Second World War.

Jo stepped out of the car, closing and locking the aluminium alloy doors.

She was wearing an ocelot fur coat and carrying a clutch bag where she kept her cigarettes and her silver 1957, *Ronson Varaframe* gas lighter and her Italian leather purse.

Her father had bought them both for her when she had first gone to Rome by train when she was in her early twenties; he smoked cigars so he only ever used matches.

She sat on a bench and put her bag on her lap. The wind ruffled her hair but the coolness revived her after her long drive. Slipping off her gloves and snapping open the bag with her free hand, she fished the car keys from the pocket of her fur and swapped them for a packet of *Senior Service.*

She pushed the bottom of the packet up to reveal sixteen cigarettes, non-filter, they looked like white candles. Extracting one and closing the box, she returned the pack to her handbag exchanging it for her lighter.

The mechanism clicked, the flint sparked and a small flame danced on the top of the open jaws of the lighter. Touching the end of the cigarette with the fire, she breathed in and the noxious, toxic fumes filled her lungs.

A rush of nicotine went straight to the receptors in her head. She exhaled luxuriantly; the smoke blowing through her nose and slightly parted lips.

Jo enjoyed smoking, knowing full well that it was bad for her health but she only smoked spasmodically on her own and on social occasions. This was the first and last she would have for that day, or so she thought at the time, twenty would last her a fortnight, usually.

When she finished the cigarette she tossed the butt down a drain and went into the cathedral. It was home to the relics of St Chad and was designated a Minor Basilica by Pope Pius XII.

Before making the sign of the cross, she dipped her fingers, middle and index, in the cold Holy water, scooping it from the stoup in the Narthex. Praying for the soul of Richard Harris, the poor man murdered in Cedar's Road she lit a candle and focused her thoughts on her prayers, it was a five-minute-meditation. She had already said the Rosary on the way up in the car.

As a child growing up in Wicklow, she had read in the newspaper about the night in November 1940 an incendiary bomb came through the Cathedral roof, bounced on the floor and exploded when it hit the central heating pipes. The pipes burst and the water extinguished the bomb, thus saving the Cathedral from destruction.

She looked at her *Longines Conquest Ladies* watch as she stepped back out into the winter sunshine. Someone was waiting for her on the steps. Peggy Donaldson, was wearing a beige wool coat that came down to her knees, she wore tan stockings and black court shoes.

To protect her brown curly hair from the wind, she wore a blue parachute silk scarf. Jo with her flyaway hair wore nothing. Peg was about five foot four and cuddly.

"Hello Peg, darling," Jo called.

"Hello, Jo, darling," replied Peg, the two old friends hugged affectionately.

Doctor Peg O'Brien was a Medical Practitioner as well.

She worked as a doctor in the Accident and Emergency department of the nearby hospital. Her lawyer husband, Roderick, was in the Cayman Islands writing the constitution for the newly independent state, their Constitution Day had been 4th July 1959, over four months ago but Roderick still needed to tie up some loose ends; dot an 'i' and cross a 't' or two. He was hoping to be back in England for Christmas to celebrate with his family and see in 1960 in England.

Peg and Jo had known each other well for over a decade and were more like sisters than friends. They walked as they talked, going back to the *Rolls*. They caught up on each other's work lives, the children and their own extended family.

Peg and Roderick had a son called Patrick, Jo asked after him as she unlocked the passenger door for her and she confirmed that her son was thriving at a nursery near the hospital.

Jo walked around the front of the car, running her hand over the *Spirit of Ecstasy* on her way to the driver's door. It was like a talisman that would bring her luck when touched.

"I'm going to drive around the town and you can tell me everything."

"Of course, as you said on the phone," Peg answered. "How was the trip up?"

"Very smooth, thank you, darling," Jo replied. She was not going to boast about doing a hundred   miles an hour.

She had done it for her on quiet satisfaction, not to brag about it. Jo loved speed, flying, ski-ing, driving big fast cars. She was a great driver despite being taught by George. George was a bit of a bully behind the wheel. He was less patient and intuitive behind the wheel.

The city was a building site; during the Second World War it had been a major manufacturing centre, and therefore obvious target for German bombing. More than two thousand people died.

Between the end of the war and nineteen-fifty-four, more than thirty thousand council houses were built but a survey in 1954 showed that twenty per cent of the houses in Birmingham were still unfit for human habitation so the council building programme had continued unabated. The bombing, the depravation, all was to be forgotten in the forward sweep of progress that would reshape the city and the inhabitants' lives. Birmingham was going to be renewed in a forward thinking modernist building programme.

Despite its problems, Peg loved the city, it had a great community feel but everyone admitted that the housing conditions were dire, which did not bode well for the health of the residents of the city. Birmingham had the largest Irish immigrant community next to Liverpool and London; it was like being at home. Most of her patients, at the Birmingham General Hospital, were Irish as were a large proportion of the staff.

"Spill the beans," Jo demanded putting on a creditable American accent, trying to sound like a hard-bitten Chicago gangster. They had both been brought up on the *Hollywood* movies.

"Okay, sweat heart," Peggy replied, sounding like James Cagney playing a violent hoodlum, she actually sounded alarmingly convincing in her role.

Jo negotiated another roundabout and pulled into a side road. Reaching under the dashboard, she pulled the handbrake on and put the gear selector in park. Switching off the engine, she looked at the clock; it was twelve forty. She had done well, getting there in just over three and a half hours.

"Now," Jo said seriously, turning to Peg, "Tell me again what you found."

"After your call last week, we had a very similar case. A man coming in with carbon monoxide poisoning, " Peggy declared, Jo looked askance, it was too much of a coincidence to mean nothing.

"I would imagine there are a stream of them from what I can gather about living conditions in some rented accommodation. It was the same in Dublin," Jo noted dryly.

"You're right but our man, John Allen, had bruises around his neck like your cadaver and there was a blow to the head," remonstrated Peg, "he reckoned it was a hammer of some sort. He was saved by a friend. His attacker was left handed."

Jo took in all this information; it certainly chimed with her victim.

"So like our 'so called suicide', your patient had been strangled, hit on the head and the gassed," Jo confirmed, shaking her head in disbelief.

"Exactly, quite a coincidence, wouldn't you say?" Peg agreed.

"Cigarette, darling, I could use one?" Jo asked, realising that she was breaking her rationing yet again.

She had promised herself she would not smoke more than her quota each day and yet this case encouraged her to smoke more. Soon she would be smoking when driving the car if she was not too careful.

"No thank you, Jo, they're bad for you, didn't you know?"

"Darling, I live in London, the pollution there will kill me long before the cigarettes do," Jo replied.

As a concession, she wound down the window before lighting up another *Senior Service*. This was one of her thinking cigarettes.

She would normally eschew smoking more than one cigarette a day. Since the murder her intake of cigarettes per week had risen considerably.

Normally, she rationed her intake of her one and only luxury purchase but on special occasions she relented and smoked more. These were mitigating circumstances as far as she was concerned.

She drew on the decorated end where the brand's emblem of a sailing ship was printed in blue on the filter paper.

They were the most expensive brand of cigarette unless you included those hand made in Haymarket by Fribourg & Treyer. The nicotine coursed through her bloodstream.

"You have a point but my drug is tea, so strong you can stand a spoon in it, I'm dying for a cuppa, now."

"Yes, with two sugars and you know sugar is a poison and affects the liver and kidneys."

"Don't tell *Coca Cola*!" Peg warned.

"Back to the case in point."

"It's relatively simple, these murders and attempted murder are connected, I'm sure there are more than just our two cases. There could be a serial killer or a gang behind it."

"And it could have remained undetected but for one thing," Jo noted mischievously.

"Exactly, we talk to each other, we discuss things properly, not in a superficial way!" Peg joked; it was one of their 'in-jokes', a comment on modern conversation.

"The fact that I know you has allowed *us* to see this connection, what about the police? They haven't made any progress"

"We naturally reported it, but the victim refused to tell the police what had happened; I only found out all the details by quizzing the nurses; our particular patient was found unconscious by his best friend just before the gas entered his bloodstream."

"That was fortunate," Jo sighed.

"Luckily, his friend had called around to see him; his motorbike was there so he broke down the door when there was no reply."

"That was lucky."

"John Allen was slumped by the gas fire but his injuries were consistent with your victim."

"That's incredible," Jo, gasped, she meant it in the literal sense of the word; she could not believe it.

"Sadly, the Metropolitan Police and the West Midlands Police don't necessarily share information, it's not like the *Garda* back home; each region polices their own area," Peg explained, she had spoken to a sergeant who regularly attended 'A and E' in a professional capacity.

"You think we should tell our respective inspectors the coincidence. Your patient…"

"John Allen," Peg reminded her.

"Sorry, John Allen was too scared to talk to the police, but he might talk to me," Jo suggested.

"Jo this is dangerous work, the people who tried to kill him might try to do you in as well," Peg warned.

"To dig I am unable, to beg I am too proud; I have no choice Peg, you know that, we signed the same oath, you and I."

"I hate to be accused of Hippocratic hypocrisy but you don't need to do this, you could leave it to the police," Peg pleaded.

"I could, but there are only two problems, they would not get as far as I can and I would be unable to sleep, knowing that I had not done my utmost to see this through."

"I understand; a woman has to do what a woman has to do," said Peg, "now, let's go somewhere and get a cup of tea."

"A splendid idea," Joe confirmed; they always agreed on the important things.

"I'd love to know how you're going to track down this John Allen," Peg admitted.

"Where did he work?" Jo asked.

"I wrote down the address the nurse remembered, it was some big company that invests in shares, here it is," Peg proudly announced.

"Well done," Jo commented admiringly. Jo would take the information to Regan and then she would be rid of the investigation and return to full time general practice. Pathology was an interesting branch of medicine but not for a wife and mother of two toddlers.

Carefully, unfolding the scrap of paper on which she had made copious notes and reading out the name, "*Global Portfolio*, he tried to get the nurse to invest!"

"You are a marvel, Peg."

"He told her he worked down the road so it's not far from the hospital."

"I'll drop you off and we'll compare notes later."

"Have a cup of tea first."

"I intend to, I'm parched. All this detective work has left me dry mouthed," Jo admitted.

Chapter Seven - The Pool Room Blues.

The Poolroom was accessed by two fire doors, one pinned open against the brick wall, and the other closed. The wide stone staircase of the warehouse led down to the area where tobacco barrels, cases of gin and whiskey or fine wined had been stored in-Bond.

The *Bonded Warehouse* had not been used since the end of the war, the business had moved to a more secure site outside town; an enterprising entrepreneur had filled the ground floor with full size pool tables in the far corner.

Jo parked the *Rolls* in a side street, folded her fur coat so the lining was showing and placed it reverently in the carpeted boot, swapping it for her pea green wool coat and wrapping a green chiffon scarf over her golden locks, she strode confidently around the corner to the entrance and walked down the steps as if she owned the place.

A fug of cigarette smoke obscured the light that was coming from the green shaded table lights, moving up to the ceiling like wisps of morning mist. Four bare light bulbs provided the only other light in the room.

The click clack of balls hit and hitting the others in the pockets, echoed through the room. It was like a tournament. Eight tables of eight ball, all played with the intensity.

These were high-stakes games, bet on by other members of the club, rent money for a week could be won on a single game, a player ruined by his loss.

The floor was occupied by people who would not have looked out of place in one of J. R. Murphy's, East End, docklands pubs: they were strong and tall, men whose muscles were hewn through hard graft and long hours lifting and carrying.

Alerted to her presence, the first table played a shot and stopped. The pool cues slammed onto the concrete floor. A wave of activity saw all cues on their handles and all players staring at the interlopers. Some of the crowd muttered about the disturbance but most just stared at Jo.

She untied her scarf and shook her hair, slipping the scarf into her coat pocket. Dipping her hand in her other pocket, she rummaged around and suddenly, in her right hand, she held a *Senior Service*, which she slipped between her lips.

She smiled at the nearest pool player.

"Have you got a light, please?" she asked, raising her eyebrow.

The man smiled, admitting to himself that whoever she was, she had nerve. Moving the cue from his right hand to left and resting it on his left shoulder, he approached her, struck a match on the back of his denim overalls and raised his hand to the cigarette end.

She inhaled deeply and turned her head, deliberately avoiding blowing smoke in his face. She thanked him and folded her arms, casually holding the cigarette in her right hand, challenging the man to fill the silence.

"What are you doing here?" he asked barely disguising his contempt. "This is a men's club."

"I want a game of pool, are you man enough to take me on?" she retorted, smoking her cigarette quickly.

"You sound a bit posh to be hanging out here, what's the story here?" the man asked, suspicion in his voice.

"I'm a doctor, I've just written a Death Certificate for a man not dissimilar to you," she informed him, looking him up and down as if sizing him up for a coffin or wondering how long he had to live, "I need distraction."

"And you want to play pool?" he asked, eyeing her with a mixture of admiration and doubt.

"I do play pool, five pounds says you won't beat me," she announced loudly so everyone could hear her challenge, taking a further drag on her cigarette and giving him a steely look with her bright blue eyes.

"Five pounds is too much for me, who the hell do you think you are?"

"Five pounds if you win, a brandy for me, if I win," she said ignoring his jibe.

His opponent, Maurice piped up from behind the table, "Go on Bert, you could do with the cash, take her on, it will be a short game. Then, we can get back to our game!"

"Bert, I'm Jo," she said, knowing that he would not be able to refuse a game, "now we know each other we can play; what do you think?"

"I think you have more money than sense. Can you give her your cue, Maurice, put some chalk on it for her would you?"

The whole pool hall formed a perimeter around the table leaving a cue's length for the players, thirty-three spectators for an early evening game was a record for that club. Jo threw the butt of her cigarette on the floor and stood on it with one of her high heels.

"Can someone take my coat?" she asked

The barman came over, there was no business, now everyone was gathered around the pool table; he locked the till and sauntered over to watch the match.

Bert was *gallant* and gave her first break.

Maurice set the frame and the balls on the table. He had been losing the game and was glad the stranger had interrupted; he had been in danger of losing four shillings. Bert should have tossed for who broke.

Jo hit the first red ball into the far side right pocket and followed with every single other ball until the table was clear. The room erupted in a tumult of applause. All the men admired how she played.

"Let's get you that brandy, Jo, you can tell, me why your really here," said the man.

"Thank you, Bert" Jo acquiesced. A brandy might be just the thing to bring her blood pressure down. It was gruelling being the only woman in the room; she could only imagine half of what they were all thinking.

The barman followed them to the bar folding her coat so the lining was showing and placing it carefully on the bar stool next to her on her right.

"What can I get you?" he asked as he lifted the hatch and stepped through.

"Bert?" Jo asked.

"It's my round," Bert protested sitting on the stool to her left.

"Bert, I need information, the pool game was just so I could get to talk to you without making it obvious. Have a drink and put your pride in your top pocket for later."

"Why talk to me?" he asked innocently. He watched as she turned to her coat and fished around for her cigarettes and change. She had left her wallet locked in the glove box of the car.

"Because, you know everyone and everything so I have been reliably informed, would you like a cigarette?"

"I've got some roll-ups."

"Indulge me, try one of these," persisted Jo, offering the pack to him,

"What will you have?"

"*Light and Mild* thanks."

While they had been talking, the bar man had poured the half pint of beer, which was in fact three quarters full and placed the half pint bottle of pale ale next to it.

A brandy in a highball glass without ice arrived seconds later followed by a soda water bottle. Jo raised her glass and sloshed soda onto the caramel coloured liquid.

"So you know, John Allen?" she asked, accepting a light from him.

"Who wants to know?" he almost spat; he was still suspicious.

"Just me, I live in London and someone was attacked in a similar way; I thought it was suicide at first but I think it was in fact, murder."

"So what's it got to do with John?"

"The attacks were similar."

"So you say," he argued.

"If they were connected, it means we have someone who is murdering indiscriminately."

"And if they weren't, you can go home."

"I need to know."

"You need to know nothing, leave it to the police. They're the best people to deal with it. Go home."

"So you won't help me?"

"I am helping you; go home. Finish your drink, go home and forget about all of this."

"It sounds like a warning to me."

"Just some friendly advice from me. Trust me you do not want to get involved with these people."

"So, I was right."

"If that's what you want to hear, so be it. Now finish your fag, drink your brandy and get lost."

"If I could."

"If, if, I'll give you if," he answered, "my Dad said if you auntie had balls she'd be your uncle. If you were meant to be a detective you wouldn't have spent all the time at medical school."

"Saving life is the same thing."

"Concentrate on what you do best, pet. Don't mess with these characters. Stay alive."

With that, he drained his glass and left.

The owner placed another brandy on the counter.

"On the house," he said smiling.

"I'm fine with the one thank you," Joe laughed, "are you trying to get me drunk?"

"Go on, I put my money on you and you've made me a fortune."

He left the drink there.

"I'm feeling a bit giddy already, I've forgotten to eat, never drink on an empty stomach," she advised.

"Never share a drink with strangers."

"Especially, bar men, you never know what they might slip into your drink."

"You are dead right, so easy for someone to slip in a Mickey Finn, I would imagine."

"Chloral hydrate?"

"Something like that, but don't worry Doctor, I'll catch you when you fall."

"I didn't tell you I was a doctor."

"You're surprisingly lucid, of course your tall, maybe I should have used a few more drops," he said, removing the two glasses from the bar.

"That's all right, I'm fighting it."

With that she put her elbows on the bar folded her arms and slumped forward onto the bar.

Chapter Eight – Driving Drugged.

I

Jo woke up in a small square room with no windows, exposed floor rafters on the ceiling and a dusty cement floor; it was just like the cellar in her house. It was possible to stand up but she was tied to a bentwood chair by some heavy ship's rope.

There was a square table under a single sixty-watt bulb suspended from a brown cord and shrouded by a metal cone shaped shade. At the table sat a man in a white shirt, a navy three piece, pinstripe suit and black brogues; next to him on the third chair sat a man in a lab coat that covered charcoal grey trousers, he was wearing black wellington boots, glasses and a frown.

"Good afternoon Doctor Murphy," he hissed with a hint of a mid-central European accent. "It is imperative you get home to your children. You must rush, put your foot down."

"Of course," she acquiesced.

"How fast were you going to get here?"

"Very fast."

You must go faster."

"Faster."

"Put your foot down."

"Foot down," she slurred drowsily.

"Faster," he implored.

"Faster."

"Put your foot right down."

"Right down," she mumbled, dribbling from the corner of her mouth, her face slack, her body limp.

"Bray, is the car outside?"

"Yes, professor."

"Help me get the doctor to her car and help me with the key words."

"Key words," Jo muttered.

"Faster, doctor, it's an emergency, faster," the professor pleaded.

"Faster, doctor," Bray demanded.

"Faster," Jo repeated.

"Put your foot down."

"Put your foot down."

"Put your foot down."

The two men hauled the limp body out of the chair and she staggered to the doorway; taking her right hand, the doctor led her up the wooden staircase to the door that led out into the street. Bray held her other hand and pushed her up the stairs. They stood on the landing and the professor pushed open the door that opened into a small courtyard. Crossing to a black metal gate, the two men supported her.

Bray pulled open the gate and she staggered through it, supported by the professor, Bray rushed ahead and opened the door of the *Rolls,* slipping the key in the ignition before helping his accomplice to settle her in the driving seat. He turned they key and started the engine. Physically pulling her right leg onto the brake, he selected drive from the stalk gear lever.

"You must go, doctor, it's an emergency, quickly" the professor whispered in her before closing the door. "Go straight, you'll find the way.

"Straight on," she mumbled in affirmation.

The men watched as she eased her foot off the break and the car slipped silently from the kerb and pulled out to the left into the empty road, the car swerved to the right and was corrected once again so it sat in the middle of the road. The speed increased, the white lines disappearing under the centre of the car, more rapidly as the car built up speed. Bray smiled at the professor and they returned behind the metal gate, which clanged shut.

ii

Her bloodstream was pumped full of a cocktail of *Benzedrine* and alcohol. Jo's foot was on the accelerator, her body was upright, her chin held high. She stared through the windscreen. Her eyes were trying to focus through the fug. She squinted through the fog in her mind. She needed to get back to London. The clock on the dashboard ticked and the houses flashed by. Time was flying by and she thought she could fly. She was flying.

She remembered what he had said.

"You're on the motorway, put you foot down."

But, who was he?

Still the clock ticked; still the buildings flashed by.

"Put your foot down!"

She crossed a junction, she glanced down; the speedometer read sixty. The clock read midnight. Miraculously, there were no cars on that road so late, that night.

"Faster."

The headlights shone, the buildings of the next street flashed by.

She marvelled at how alert she was, at how smoothly the car was driving.

"Put your foot down."

Ahead was the dead end; on the other side of the wall was the cemetery.

Still the buildings flashed by; still the clock ticked.

"Faster, faster," he had urged. "You have to get back to London, quickly, go faster.

The wall grew closer, she could hear the tick, so clearly; she could see the wall so clearly.

Everything was so bright, every sound was enhanced and the smell of leather was so strong.

"Faster," he had exclaimed encouragingly.

She felt she could see over the wall.

Once she was through the wall, the road would be straight.

"Faster," he insisted in her head.

Not long now, she would be at the wall and through. The wall would not stop her getting back to George. Once she was through the wall it would be a short trip.

The wall, the wall, the wall, it was coming closer and closer and closer.

A wall!

What had he said? "Put your foot down!"

A wall!

"Faster, Jo, go faster!"

A brick wall!

"Put your foot down."

She did.

She stamped her foot down.

There was a screech; the hydraulic brakes bit. The servo-assisted drums locked. The car ground to a halt. The sudden cessation of motion meant the bodywork lurched forward; the chrome bumper hit the wall with a clang.

"Faster, Jo, go faster."

The car had stopped the bumper just brushing the brickwork.

"Put your foot down."

Jo slumped over the steering wheel, which she had used to brace herself.

'Who was he?' she wondered.

Her mind was clear, she felt alert, awake; the *Benzedrine* was working. The amphetamine was beating the depressant influence of the alcohol, now, it was beginning to have its proper euphoria inducing effect.

Benzedrine had been given to RAF pilots to keep them awake on nighttime bombing missions. After the war, it had become one of the earliest synthetic stimulants. The drug had made her high. However, the alcohol was still making her feel fuggy. Jo could not remember how she had got into the car, how before that she had been slipped the *Benzedrine*; had been plied with alcohol and had been hypnotised to drive at breakneck speed, through two junctions, driving towards the wall.

The alcohol was a depressant the Benzedrine was a stimulant; they fought inside her body and fought inside her head. Still slumped forward, she took the keys from the ignition. She sat upright and stared ahead at the wall. She could have been killed; she should have been killed.

Thoughts of her mother, her father, her brothers and sisters and of course George had somehow entered her addled brain a split second before it would have been too late. Any other car would have smashed into the wall and the engine block would have been forced into the passenger compartment; a mobile object meeting a stationary object at speed would have had the force equivalent to an elephant hitting a tree trunk. Neither would survive.

The only thing that saved her life was the servo-assisted brakes and the sudden realisation that the wall was an immobile obstacle. Shaken, she staggered from the driver's seat, opened the back door and lay across the bench seat at the back of the car. She curled up on the cool leather and waited for sleep to sweep over her. It did not take long; she had only just closed her eyes when she found herself in the arms of Morpheus.

Chapter Nine – i - The Proposal

"Are you insane?" asked Derek Bannister.

"Certainly, you could argue that but we think you will be quite happy with the performance your company makes when it is listed," Arthur Bray replied

"You're asking me to promote Matthew Andrews to the post?"

"Of course," Bray responded casually, he located his gold *Colibri Stormgard* lighter in his waistcoat, fumbled for his *Benson and Hedges* cigarettes, "Would you care for a cigarette?"

"Thank you, but Mary Baines is far more qualified and more suitable for the job, she's been doing the same role in Hong Kong for five years; Andrews is a blow in, hardly been with us a year. The shareholders won't like it," Bannister argued.

"You'll have to sell the idea to them, then, unless you want to be looking for a job next year with a worthless share portfolio." Bray warned, proffering the pack and, once the cigarette was taken, snapping his lighter into life.

"Is that a threat?" Bannister asked, taking the light proffered and inhaling deeply as he gave Bray a steely stare.

"More of promise, I would say, my colleagues would prefer if you were taken out of the picture all together. You may have read about such matters, there has been a spate of poor unfortunates poisoning themselves with gas."

"You don't expect me to believe you were responsible for all those deaths, do you?" asserted Bannister.

"No, but all those were single men, your friend Tim, what was his name?"

"Gibbons."

"Yes, unfortunate accident, he   had children just like you."

"So I'm going to meet with a fatal accident on my way to one of the factories?" asked Banister.

"I sincerely hope not."

"Good, Mary gets the job."

"You miss my point, we cannot allow women into these high ranking posts, we'll have to pay them the same as men, it will not do."

"That will never happen."

"I should hope not; what we're doing here is saving the establishment; we can't have competent women coming on board, making us look slipshod and amateurish," Bray argued.

"So, you and your friends are petrified that the rise of women in the workforce will threaten your cosy jobs, is that it?"

"In a nutshell, you must see we cannot let them loose in the boardroom or in management."

"The world would be a far more pleasant and productive place, judging by Mary's record in Hong Kong, even her rivals adore her."

"That's precisely what we want to avoid, up to now, we have only targeted the men who have suggested promoting women, if the women are in post we will have to execute them."

"Did I hear you right?"

"I never said a word, dear boy, remember Europe is being built out the ashes. Remind me when rationing ended."

"You know as well as I do, 4th July 1954."

"Precisely, over nine years after war; do we want to measure our progress in decades?"

"But women will help the process or rebuilding as they helped in the war effort."

"Yes, yes, of course but we don't want an equal world and a fair workplace for women. We want them to have children not careers. We'll never be safe once the women take over."

"You're serious," Bannister interjected.

"Deadly."

"And if I don't comply with your wishes?"

"I cannot hold back my colleagues, they will take the action that they see fit."

"Who are they?"

"Never you mind, suffice to say, you and Mary will not be on their Christmas card list and that, my dear boy, is not good news."

"You're all mad."

Bray leant forward and stubbed out his cigarette in the round green glass ashtray that stood in the corner of the desk. Bannister was only half way through his.

"Without a shadow of a doubt. Now what's your answer?" he agreed.

"I would be made not to promote Mary."

"Wrong answer. You'll have until I finish my second cigarette to come up with the right one," announced Bray, extracting a cigarette from packet and lighting it. He returned the pack to his inside jacket pocket and the lighter to his waistcoat, took a greedy drag on his cigarette before he stared at Bannister with cold, calculating eyes before releasing the smoke from behind his teeth, blowing the smoke away from his victim's face.

"Okay, I know what happened to the Stephen."

"And Charles."

"Charles Wood, you didn't?"

"I want everyone to realise we are serious."

"You win, who would you like appointed in her place?"

"My man of course."

"I suppose Andrews will do a reasonable job."

"Then it's agreed."

"One thing, can Mary be his assistant."

"Why of course, she can do all the hard work and he can get the credit; \we have never objected to that."

"It was ever thus," admitted Bannister, smiling grimly and sitting back in his chair.

"You made the right choice," Bray soothed.

Both of them knew that a life had   been saved that day.

Chapter Nine – ii - Having a Ball

George was propping up the bar in the Rembrandt, he fancied himself as an Irish Cary Grant mixed with John Wayne, he was ruggedly handsome, tall with blue eyes, a high brow and thick black hair gave him the vague air of a Hollywood film idol, but his ears and nose were too big for him to be truly handsome, but still enough of the ladies in the bar turned their heads and gave him approving appraisal or even a smile.

He was happy, he was a successful surgeon, he had a Harley Street practise and the fledgling health service paid him for his clinics at St. Mary's Paddington or St George's Hyde Park Corner and the Tooting hospital of the same name in the afternoon. Through that he had picked up some private patients. His wife worked, too, they had two houses and three holidays a year, ski-ing, The Riviera and Ireland. Not bad for a boy from Mayo.

Dressed in black tie, patent shoes, he looked elegant and sophisticated. He still looked as fit as he did when he played rugby for Balinrobe. He was well-educated and even more importantly well-read; he could quote Shakespeare, recite poetry and play the piano, a shinning example of how good education can produce a witty and erudite individual.

"Darling," Jo said at his shoulder as she caught him looking in the mirror first at himself and then at a brunette in a dark green dress smoking a cigarette through a dark green cigarette holder that seemed to be a foot long.

"Darling," he replied, "there's a woman over there with a blow dart pipe, watch out."

"Clearly, you are on watch yourself, I shall be keeping an eye on you so you had better watch out, too."

"Darling, I only have eyes for you, my sweet."

"Sweets to my sweet, can you get me a drink, please, darling, I'm parched."

"What would you like?"

"Surprise me."

"I'm having a Bloody Mary."

"We've only been here together five minutes and you're already swearing. I'll have a whisky and soda, I think, I prefer my B.M.s as a starter for lunch, a tomato soup."

"Whisky and soda it is?"

"*Quel Surprise,* is that the most imaginative you can be, I'll have a *pastis* if they have it, brandy and ginger if not."

"I love that dress."

"The *Balmain*, thank you darling and you look so handsome in your penguin outfit."

"It's *Chester Barrie* from *Harrod's*," he announced proudly.

"I know, I bought it for you."

"And it fits like a glove."

"42 long and 34, 34, a mannequin's figure."

"36, 24, 34, a model figure."

"Flatterer."

"Credit where credit due, you look gorgeous tonight."

"And you are the most handsome man in the room but if I see you looking at the girl with the green proboscis again, I shall perform surgery on your nether regions."

"Forewarned is forearmed."

"There's a good boy, you will be rewarded and that, my love, is a promise."

"Who's that talking to Harold Clowes and the Fitzherberts?" asked George, raising a glass of red wine to his lips.

"Not a clue, darling, why, does he have a stigmatism that needs sorting out?" Jo asked.

"He might well do," chortled George, "it's just that I recognise him, I think he was on the health committee at St Mary's."

"Lots of businessmen are, shall we find out?"

Jo approached Sir Harold Clowes who had become Lord Mayor of the city of Stoke-on Trent; they had met in Grasse four years ago and he had hitched a ride in Jo and George's *1937 MG* and they had toured the Italian Riviera and the Amalfi coast together on; he had subsequent trips.

"Jo, darling," how are you?"

"Very well, how are you, darling?"

"All the better for seeing you!"

"My what big eyes you have."

And here comes the big bad wolf, how are you George?"

"Mad, bad and dangerous to know, you look well," George replied, smiling broadly with a twinkle in his eyes.

"Never better, must be the Cotes de Blaye they serve here."

"How is the Bentilee project coming along?"

"It's now officially the largest social housing project in Europe, we're going to be building 4,500 homes in all."

"Well then!"

"Fairly, how are things is the world of ophthalmic surgery?"

"I'm coping with the cut and thrust."

"I see!"

"Very busy, but enjoying it all."

"That's good news; let me introduce you to Bray, he's known as the pie man not because he's got the same girth as me but because he has his fingers in so many."

"Doctor Jo and Doctor George Fitzpatrick, let me introduce you Arthur Bray esquire, entrepreneur and philanthropist, this ball was his idea."

"A great cause."

"I hope we can persuade you to dig deeper when we start the auction, later tonight. So you are both doctors, Harold tells me."

"You are well informed."

"He was telling me about your last jaunt to Rapallo."

"And where did you go for your holiday?"

"Nowhere as glamorous, Scotland, my mother has a place near Glencoe, I like to wash away the cement with a bit of salmon fishing."

"So you provide the cement for Bentilee."

"It's one of my business interests; I believe your father was responsible for the building of the new monastery at Nunraw Abbey."

"Do you know Lammermuirs?"

"Only through the glass company that supplied the materials for the new abbey, I haven't been there. I believe it is the first monastery built in the UK since *The Reformation*."

"Did Harold Clowes tell you that too?"

"No, I have done quite a bit of research," Bray replied.

"What on earth for?"

"Let's just say to avoid a repeat of Birmingham."

"You do have your grubby paws in plenty of pies, don't you? Do I take this as a warning."

"How are your three children, Catherina, Georgina and Patrick, is it?"

"Very well thank you."

"Good, no illnesses at present."

"None."

"Well, let's keep it that way."

"You have been busy ferreting away."

"Your father and mother alive and well in Ewell? What's the name of their home, *Fernbank*?"

"You've made your point."

"Good, as long as we understand each other."

"Perfectly."

"Then, all will be well."

"Will you excuse me?" Jo asked.

"Of course, it's been a pleasure."

"Oh, no," Jo hissed sarcastically, "the pressure was all mine."

"There's a good girl, I do not think any further action is needed at this stage, would you agree?"

"Agreed," she whispered, fury in her eyes.

"Harold has gone off to meet and great the great and the good. What have you two been talking about?" asked George, "What's wrong?"

"Arthur and I were just discussing building houses for the poor, you know how incensed I get about injustice."

"Oh, yes, Jo used to visit the poor in Dublin when she was in college there and went to visit people in hospital," George announced proudly.

"I was just saying how she is a living saint."

"More a sinner than a saint," Jo added brightly, hiding her feelings.

"A saint is a dead sinner, revised and edited, Ambrose Bierce said," George noted."

"And he is?" asked Bray.

George was delighted to inform him.

"The author of An Occurrence at Owl Creek Bridge, the civil war writer."

"Yes, dying with dignity," Jo added.

"Precisely," said Bray .

"Jo, shall we dance?" George suggested.

"What a spelndid, idea, darling," she responded.

"Will you excuse us Arthur?" George said.

He had picked up on the charged atmosphere. As Jo used to say, you could have 'cut the atmosphere with a knife.

"Of course, I hope to see you after the auction."

"I love to dance, see you later in the evening, Mr. Bray."

"Perhaps you will honour me with a dance later?"

"I only dance with partners who are taller than me, I'm afraid, it's a rule I stick to rigidly."

With that remark she hooked her arm into Geroge's and headed for the Dorchester dancefloor.

"What was that all about?" George asked.

"A few mysonginist comments and a threat to the children and my parents."

"Let's go and talk."

"Dance first and then talk."

"Your wish is my command."

George could resist everything but temptation and his tempatation at that stage in his life was Jo and Jo alone.

\

On a cold and frosty morning, before dawn, a car coughed into life, its headlights flicked on at the touch of a switch and the full beam cut through the morning mist swirling in the twilight. John Rickard Murphy drove his *Rover P5* out of the garage at *Fernbank.*

Assiduously, he wiped the windscreen with a chamois cloth, there was no frost on the window but moisture had collected on the windscreen. Francis Cahill, his stock taker and fellow director, walked out of the kitchen door.

"Bridget, has cooked you some chicken to have for your lunch, she said swinging a wicker basket in her right hand.

With her left hand, she pushed the button on the unlocked boot and lifted it, before popping the basket into the boot. Underneath, the Irish linen table cloth was a whole roasted chicken, three boiled eggs in their shells and nestled in the bottom a fresh baked cottage loaf and a butter dish filled with *Kerrygold* butter brought over on the Liverpool steamer by a friend of Bridget's. Bridget has been Kitty and John's cook for ten years. She was a jolly character, an excellent cook and a wonderful woman.

Francis had joined the company in 1940 at the height of the *Battle of Britain* during the *Blitz*. She was from Cork, she talked quickly and her mental arithmetic was legendary; she could do a stock take in the time it would take two men to complete the same task, she would be right and they would be out by at least a pound. She would find their error for them and leave them red faced and amazed.

"I was going to have lunch with the Blooms," J.R. complained, looking at Francis as she walked around to the driver's door.

"You are having lunch with them tomorrow, Mr Murphy," Francis corrected him as she watched the old man walk around and open the passenger door.

"Oh, it's Tuesday today, I was a day ahead again, I must be getting old or stupid one or the other," he noted.

"Or both," Francis suggested.

"Yes," he admitted, "but there's a third thing, too, I'm getting impatient with my children, too, where is Michael?"

"Here he is."

"What time did you come in from *The French House* last night."

"I'm not sure, Francis, was it quarter to our quartet past?"

"Get in the back seat and make sure you don't do any backseat driving," Francis commanded and when Francis commanded, Michael and Doctor John and JR obeyed.

She eased the *Rover* onto the Cheam Road. The Ford parked opposite the house started its engine. Inside sat two men who were both dressed in grey trilby hats, navy raincoats and charcoal suits. They were in no rush, they waited for the car they would be following to gather a pace before following.

"Is that the target vehicle?" asked the driver.

"What are you on about, you've been watching too many films, that's the car we should be following, yes, a *Rover P5*, registration *JRM6*. There can't be many of them around.

"I would reckon maybe six," suggested the driver as he eased his car onto the main road and accelerated in pursuit.

"They won't all be blooming *Rovers* will they smart Alec? Use your noggin, this must be the only one driving so early in the morning."

"So where are we headed?"

"If they are creatures of habit which most people are and if our information is correct, six o'clock mass at St. Anselm's next to Tooting Bec tube followed by a drive along the south bank to number one Whitechapel Road."

"What's that then?"

"A pub."

"I could do with a pint."

"They won't be open at ten will they numbskull."

"I can wait an hour."

Francis drove the *P5* expertly, it was a 1958, three litre, straight six with an overhead intake valve and side exhaust valves, which meant she was very powerful and quick. Changing gear was taken care of by the automatic transmission and it even had *Burman* power steering, unusual in those days in English cars. The brakes were *Girling* drums, which took a bit of getting used to and yet in the October 1959 London Motor Show disc brakes were employed for the first time.

They had brought the car a year too soon. If Jo had been driving the Rover, she would have crashed through the wall not stopped at it.

The Ford followed Michael J.R., Michael and Francis, parking in Cambridge Heath Road on the opposite side to the *Rover.* Watching as the trio entered the side door that led up to the offices, the two men said nothing. The navy raincoats bought themselves a bacon sandwich from a café on Whitechapel Road and waited for the pub on Mile End road to open.

J.R. bottled his own Guinness straight from Dublin. It was rumoured to be less bitter than the Guinness that they had been pumping out from Guinness in Park Royal since 1938. The word on the street was that it was 'a taste of sweet, creamy Guinness from home'.

On Sunday, George parked the *Rolls* outside *The Atheneum Club* and stared up at the one hundred and twenty four foot Duke of York Column, seeing the back of Prince Frederick, Duke of York, the second eldest son of King George III.

Being inquisitive he knew the designer was Benjamin Dean Wyatt. He wondered when they would open up the staircase and allow people up; they would get a wonderful view of *Admiralty Arch* and *Horseguards*.

Taking Catherina's hand, he led the eight year old from the passenger seat net to him, closed the door and opened up the back door to allow Georgina and Patrick to propel themselves off the leather upholstery and to the carpeted edge where their father lifted them down onto the road. All cars were parked at forty-five degrees to the pavement, in bays helpfully marked out by Westminster Council.

"Now, you three, best behaviour on the pavement, hold hands tightly," George demanded his Irish brogue, grabbing his eldest daughter's hand, "I don't want to stop coming here do I?"

"No, daddy," Catherina agreed readily, smiling at her father.

"I wouldn't mind too much," Georgina muttered precociously.

"Are you swimming with us today?" asked Patrick hopefully.

"After my massage," promised George, having no intention of setting foot in the pool. This was his time, a massage, sauna and then a pint of milk. "I've arranged a swimming lesson for you."

"Thank you, daddy," they all chorused in unison.

They had been to Majorca for their holidays, and were desperate to learn to swim although Georgina would be as content with a book. The pavement on Pall Mall was wide and despite the fact that the trio had a combined age of twenty, they made swift progress, helped by their father's long strides and the skipping girls forcing the youngest boy to run along behind, barely managing to keep hold of Georgina's hand.

They passed The Reform Club, The Traveller's Club and George could see flag for the Royal Automobile Club, flapping in the wind. Above him, the smog had not yet settled over London but given time, he knew that it would. In his mind he was walking through the revolving doors and walking down the spiral staircase to the pool so when a man stood in front of him, George he was perturbed. He stopped and the children sensing a slackening of the rope that bound them, stopped, too.

"Excuse me Doctor," said Tweed.

"Good morning," George replied, racking his brain, it would not have been the first time a grateful patient had stopped him in the street and thanked him for saving their sight or providing excellent treatment, he was a specialist and a perfectionist in his professional life. "Can I help you?"

"It is I who can help you. Perhaps we should talk in the club?"

"What's it about."

"Your family, of course, I wouldn't be bothering you on a Sunday morning if it were not of vital importance."

"I'm with the children today."

"Yes but for how much longer?"

"You can reach me at 186 Harley Street, I'm there at six thirty, my clinics start at seven."

"Very well, I thought we could do things the easy way."

"If it's the easy way you want, I should take that; the club only allows members."

"Really?"

"Check their policy with the doorman if you do not believe me. I could invite you for lunch but you would have to hang around for three hours and sadly I have a reservation elsewhere with the family."

"Very well, enjoy the swim children."

"Thank you, Mr?"

"Tweed."

"Have a good day, Mr Tweed."

"Oh, I intend to doctor."

Mr Tweed crossed the road and headed towards St James's Square.

"Who was that man, daddy?" Georgina asked, "I didn't like the way he looked at you."

"I don't know, come on little ones, the pool awaits," George jovially responded.

As he watched the man move along Pall Mall, he noticed him consulting his watch. It was not on the left hand as it should have been but it was strapped to his right wrist and the face was placed over the radius and ulna where a pulse would be taken. George had only ever come across two three cases of such an affected way of wearing a watch, on all occasions, they had been left handed pugilists, boxers brought up on the street, one had been from the Repton Club in London's east end. All of them had been treated by George for damage to their eyes from a fist.

'Was Tweed, a similar south-paw, who made his living with his hands?' he wondered.

His message had been anything but cryptic; he wanted to cause someone harm and George immediately connected him to the Murder on Cedars Road.

Chapter Eleven – Mass Paranoia

Jo waited for the woman to walk past her before going out into the aisle, the smell of incense and candle wax filled her nose even though there was no *thurible* in sight. Perhaps it was a lingering smell from Benediction, the evening before.

The tranquillity of the church helped her remain calm and the total immersion in the rhythm of the service was comforting. It was her only chance in a busy week to be *still*: to think about her spirit, to reflect on her blessings and forget all her worries.

She walked towards the altar where the other members of the congregation were filing up the aisle, others came back in a minutely choreographed display, Jo followed as if mesmerised. Her footsteps matched those of the person ahead, left foot forward, right foot forward, stop as if the two of them were practising a dance step. They repeated the movement as the flow preceded them.

Once past the Pews, Jo was able to walk to the right, step forward towards the altar, waiting for a kneeling parishioner to cross herself and exit stage left. As the figure passed her, she knelt down and waited for the priest. He was working his way down the line. She closed her eyes and prayed while the priest approached. She heard the whispered exchange next to her, felt the sudden movement of the departure of the person next to her and she was ready. The host was offered to her.

"Corpus Christi," the priest intoned in a hushed voice as if sharing a secret.

"Amen," she replied before opening her mouth and pushing her tongue forward.

The host was placed on her tongue; it felt warm and hard like a piece of card; she closed her mouth over the flat white disc. Immediately, it cleaved to the top of her mouth, wet paper sticking to the bottom of a glass. Her tongue rolled over the roof of her mouth to cement the wafer there and let it dissolve,   slowly.

Crossing herself, she rose from her kneeling position, feeling a presence at the right shoulder, she moved off to the left to make way for another celebrant.

Her eyes on the floor, she walked back to her pew. A man stood up and let her into place; she knelt and prayed, she felt elated, grateful for everything she had, her soul soared and her heart filled with rapture. This was the communion. This was communing with the life essence that provides the will to live, the life to love and the life of love. She was at one with the universe.

At the end of the service, the priest intoned, "Ite missa est."

The congregation bowed their heads for the blessing also in Latin.

As she left the mass after the blessing, following the priest out of the door, she saw Anthony Bray sitting on a pew. Of course, she did not recognise him but he was staring at her with a look that emanated evil and she shuddered as she passed him.

Chapter Twelve - i - Car Crash

After Sunday mass was over, Jo climbed into the driver's seat of the 1942, *600 Ambassador 6, Slipstream Sedan* parked in Nightingale Square. It was a four door with the back door opening forward like the old classic cars from the movies but that was all that was old-fashioned about her; she was sleek and elegant. Jo admired her lines and her American opulence, the Americans loved their cars and it showed. Her *Nash* was like an old friend; her father bought it for her when she passed her examinations into *The Royal College of Surgeons*.

She had been the only person to own a car apart from the Dean, his was a pre-war *Austin*; hers was a sleek two-tone beauty, a navy blue body and a midnight blue roof with white-wall tyres. The *Nash* was one of the last cars to come off the production line before the American factory turned its focus to wartime production. It had been impossible to buy a car from England or Europe due to all factories being used to help the war effort. The only way to get a car was to have it shipped from America to Ireland.

The *600 Nash* was so named due to it being able to complete six hundred miles on one tank of petrol. It came in useful when she was visiting George in Mayo. The huge bumper at the front wrapped around the front of the chassis like a chrome smile, the football-sized headlamps guarded the five chrome lines that adorned the radiator.

The engine cowling started off like a fireman's helmet with the *Nash* badge sweeping back and widening to meet the sloping windscreen divided into two sections, which made it look like the cockpit of a streamlined plane. The boot swept down to the back bumper like a beetle; they termed it a fastback. Easing herself into the leather bench seat, she was confronted by the wonderful smell of quality hide and a chrome dashboard with two gauges that looked like clocks on either side of the speedometer that went up to 120 mph, the numbers of each decade of speed were picked out in white. She had grown fond of her comfortable and stylish car and its sophisticated switches and dials.

Above those, was a beautiful dashboard cover in dark brown, polished wood like the hull or a nineteen thirties racing yacht. The white steering wheel was thin and elegant. Just like the *Rolls* the gear lever was mounted on the steering column behind the steering wheel, unlike the *Rolls*, she was a three-speed manual with overdrive. The six cylinder purred into life when she turned the ignition, the 2.8 litre engine ticked over laconically, humming beautifully.

Easing out from the pavement, she passed three parked cars, south London was changing; cars were becoming more commonplace.

There were a number of cars in garages but the streets were fairly car free. She weaved through the backstreets, turning on to Endlesham Road; she drove across Nightingale Lane then turned left into Thurleigh Road and right into Wroughton Road.

She was four minutes away from home.

She slowed as she approached Roseneath Road, a green *Bedford* truck with a canvas-covered flatbed was parked; she could see the stationary headlamps as she approached the junction. Out of the corner of her right eye, she saw a flash of movement. That was the last thing she remembered.

The truck seven ton *Bedford S Type RL* truck thudded into the side of the car, the drivers door was crushed, the windscreen split and cracked as if hit by a stone, her driver's window shattered, the doors rumpled like a concertina.

Still the truck rolled on, its six cylinder, 4.9 litre engine providing the power; it was accelerating not breaking, sweeping the car against the pavement like a snowplough.

The car hit the kerb. The right-hand-side of the car was lifted into the air. The all four wheels of the truck were still spinning; the *RL* was four-wheel drive. A man ran out of his house, climbed up onto the cab of the truck and tore the driver's door open, pulling the driver from the seat.

The truck engine stalled as the driver's foot was removed from the accelerator; the truck gave one final lurch as the engine died, buffeting the car for the last time, the car swayed on its chassis for the last time. Jo had been thrown across the car, slipping across the bench seat, if she had been in an ordinary car she could have been killed. Thankfully, the American car was built like a tank.

Her head hit the passenger door but the panel was padded on the inside, which cushioned the contact, the slide across the seat had taken out most of momentum of the impact and the subsequent battering of the car merely bounced her on the bench like a rag doll.

She had curled into a ball as soon as she realised she was travelling across the bench seat, protecting her arms and legs and minimising the chance of injury to her organs.

Through the smashed window she heard the engine of the truck choking and dying, she felt the car being released from the constant battering and settling into a stationary wreck.

"What are you doing?" a man's voice asked.

"I thought I was braking," replied another voice.

"Really?" asked the first voice. She heard footsteps. "Where are you going, hey, come back, hey you can't leave the scene of an accident. What are you doing? Come back."

Jo heard the ambulance arriving as the man who had challenged the driver, opened the passenger door.

"Help's on its way," he assured her kindly. "The driver's run off but the police will catch him."

The 1957 *Austin LD Wandsworth* ambulance parked behind the wreckage of the Nash. The ambulance men stepped out from the front and approached the car. Just as they reached the passenger door, a police car arrived. It was a black *1956 Wolseley 6/90*, which was a controversial police car even at the time, it could barely reach 96 mph for a start and its designer Gerald Palmer was sacked and replaced by Alec Issigonis, designer of the *Min*i.

If Jo had been in the front seat of that car, it would have been curtains for her.

The police sergeant switched off the flashing blue lights using a black flick switch on the grey striped *Formica* instrument panel. The blue lights mounted on the large chrome mesh 'cheese-cutter', speaker grille went dark. Pulling on the hand brake control under the dash to the side of the steering column, he moved the column mounted gear lever to neutral. The leather trimmed front seats were mounted closely together, which would have stopped Jo on her trajectory from one side of the car to the other.

The second assassination attempt had failed only because the bench seat allowed her body to slide out of harm's way. That and the fact that the Tweed twins had not taken into account the car was left hand drive.

Jo was treated in the back of the ambulance and sat in the back of the *Wolseley* to give her details. They policemen then drove her off to her local General Practitioner who had readily offered to open his surgery to see his old friend after her accident.

ii

It was still Sunday, George was back from Pall Mall and dropped Jo off at their friend's surgery. She sat in the front room of the house that wrapped around Lavender Sweep and Battersea Rise. It was simply furnished with a desk, two chairs, on either side, and an examination bed. A desk light, plain lining paper walls in cream, a net curtain and a beige blind rolled up at the top of the wide window. The surgery was warmed by a two-bar electric heater. There was an optician's Snellen chart on the wall adjacent to the treatment table. Jo sat on the cushioned seat of the examination table, which was covered in red plastic. Her feet dangled over the edge.

Doctor Martin Walsh stood in front of her. Like her, he was Irish, he was from Cork; like her, he had established a practice in south London; like her, he was an exceptional and thorough doctor with a charming bedside manner. They had become firm friends, Anne his wife spent evenings together with Jo and George, chatting, smoking, drinking and dancing. On the occasion of Jo's visit he was looking serious, peering over his glasses.

"Jo you've had a nasty bash in that American car of yours; you were lucky it was made so solid or you might not be here," he explained, making some notes in his book, to conclude his examination.

Jo sat up on his examining couch, her silk cream camisole covered her brassiere and corset; she had kept on her skirt and stockings during the examination. She had bruises on her arms, a lump above her temple but apart from that she seemed unscathed. She had suspected a fractured left wrist, such was the pain but was relieved to find that on manipulation the wrist could be moved without pain and it was just a sprain.

Martin wore his stethoscope around his neck and a pen in one hand, his notebook in the other; the other instruments that he used to examine her were spread on his desk: sphygmomanometer, auriscope, nasal speculum, ophthalmoscope and percussion hammer.

"My lovely car, gone," Jo complained.

"It might have been you," Martin exclaimed.

"I'm fine, I just need a cigarette and a brandy."

Martin put down his notebook and fishing in his suit jacket, he silently proffered his cigarette case and when Jo had taken one, a *Player's Navy Cut,* the only other brand she would consider smoking. He lit her cigarette with a silver *Zippo*, petrol lighter, the only one he found reliable when out walking.

"It's time to give up the investigation, Jo," he insisted.

"So they have got to you have they, Martin?" Jo replied, drawing on her cigarette, it had been a hard day.

"No one's got to me Jo, you're not in a film noir, this isn't some melodrama, that's twice you have cheated death. Those drugs would have weakened a horse and you managed to stop before they wiped you out, now they've rammed you with a three-ton truck. They might be successful next time, third time lucky. Think of the children, Jo; I would never do anything to jeopardise Madeline and John."

"I'm thinking of all the children and all the parents, too. These people have murdered three people that we know of."

"Let the police deal with the situation. You should be concentrating on your job," he insisted.

"They are the one who have asked me to help them and frankly this is the second attempt at my life so I don't feel like letting it go."

"These men are dangerous, their attempts on your life cannot be ignored; they mean business. I got a call from George at the RAC before you arrived; they've threatened George and the children as well. They've also talked to Anne and I, it's a rum business."

"They seem to have influence everywhere but that doesn't mean they cannot be stopped."

"What would you like me to do?" he asked, still feeling reluctant to get involved but she left him no choice, they were old friends, they had arrived in the early fifties and were fellow General Practitioners.

"Give me a prescription for some Benzadrine and reassure Anne that all will be well."

"I can do both those things. Anything else?"

"I think we can have this case sewn up soon."

"You're lucky you weren't sewn up today. I still want you to have that wrist x-rayed."

"It's fine, don't worry."

"I do worry, this is a dangerous game you are playing."

"We're winning though," Jo assured him.

She was always confident about our abilities.

"You and Regan."

"That's right."

"Is the Benzedrine to keep you awake?"

"If you say so."

"I must remind you about the dangers of mixing them with alcohol; you are aware of the high you can get."

"I think that is the combination that led me to almost crash the car. They plied me with booze and a cocktail of hallucinogens."

"Sounds like it's personal, maybe you should see this through to the end."

"Thanks Martin."

"Let me know if you need anything. Anne and I will do what we can."

"Thank you, I know Martine and John will be fine, they aren't monsters, they wouldn't target children."

"Their track record is not good, didn't you say Peg had found a victim, they seem to be all over the country and I fear you've only discovered the tip of the iceberg."

"I can't sit by and watch them get away with this."

"I know your Hippocratic oath demands that you do all you can to save life but it does not include putting your life in danger. You have three children and a loving husband and they all rely on you and need you to survive."

"Regan's put some men on our door, they've tried twice, I doubt whether they will try again."

"You're thinking of lightning, you know the adage of the third light, one, raise rifle, two, take aim, three, fire."

"We're not in the trenches but I take your point, I'll keep my head down."

Chapter Thirteen – Finding the Flaws

"So Mr. Bray, how are you dealing with the good doctor; she seems to be popping up all over the place and your attempts to get rid of her have failed spectacularly."

"Just bad luck, in Birmingham, she came around for some reason, I blame the professor for not giving her enough of the cocktail. As for the car crash; the buffoon driving the truck was the wrong person for the job."

"Oh, how?"

"He drove the truck into the car that was left hand drive, if he'd hit her from the other side, she would have been crushed like a brazil nut in a nut cracker."

"I appreciate your seasonal analogy but seriously, do you expect me to believe your feeble excuses. I heard you had the Tweed twins working for you, I thought these two were hardened criminals, thugs of the highest water and gangsters of the highest order, they seem incompetent beyond belief and as for your absent minded professor, he forgot to drug her sufficiently. Really, did he take his pharmacy examinations?"

"He thought she would be as high as a kite on the *Benzadrine* and alcohol; he toned down the dose because she was a woman. Anyone shorter and lighter would have been a complete zombie and driven straight into the wall. It was a miracle she did not crash."

"That professor of yours is an idiot, no wonder he was struck off."

"Yes, she is a giant and so he should have given her a full adult dose and she is a doctor so she can drink like a fish, plus she's Irish. He should have tripled the dose."

"I would laugh at your amusing observations if it was not so serious. The committee wants results and they want them, now."

"The professor has learnt his lesson, a week off the laudanum was enough penance, he won't make the same mistake twice. The Tweed twins are currently reminding Jo what might happen to her father if she doesn't mind her own business, if that fails we go for the children."

"Go for the children, now."

"Let's do it my way, for now."

"With your record so far?"

"Look, the twins have done a good job so far, they're the ones who will hang if things go wrong."

"As a lawyer, I must remind you of a small matter of guilt by association."

"They have not been caught yet."

"With your Doctor snooping around, the possibility is getting closer, you have to warn her off or get rid of her."

"Without attracting too much attention. Regan knows about the trip to Birmingham and they are searching for the driver who smashed up her car."

"Whichever Tweed it was, he was Tweedle Dumb; let's hope that the 'D' in Tweedle Dee, does not stand for Tweedle Dunce or was it merely his grade in English at 'O' level "

"They'll keep Jo at bay, never you mind."

"Jo, she sounds like a friend of yours."

"Didn't I tell you, I met her at the ball to raise money for Harold Clowes's project Bentilee."

"No women in the construction industry thank God."

"Hard helmets and French waves don't go together, thankfully."

"Save the nineteen-forties imagery, please. Get the job done; we can't have women getting above their station, just because a few of them flew *Spits* from airfield to airfield doesn't mean they should climb to the rarefied atmosphere of the boardroom."

iii

Meanwhile, Jo had picked me up from the police station on Lavender Hill. A couple of constables gave me a second look as I climbed into the brown Rolls, at the back of the station, in Kathleen Road. The car smelt of warm leather and *Guerlain*, it was fast become my favourite smell.

She looped around to the traffic lights that led into Elspeth Road but she took a left past, Battersea Town Hall, and drove towards the Wandsworth Road crossing the tail end of Cedar's Road. We both looked at each other at the junction.

We chatted about our respective factories as we drove onto to Vauxhall and from there to Lambeth Palace. Driving the *Rolls* over Lambeth Bridge, I explained about the new victim who had been taken to Horseferry Road Coroner's Court.

"Three of the same type of deaths; how did you know?" Jo asked.

"As you know Coroner's Courts investigate sudden or unexplained deaths. There are only twelve in London, so I asked them to call should any of their customers came in with the same symptoms, such as suicide " I elucidated.

"You're a veritable Sherlock Holmes," Jo admitted admiringly, steering the car around the roundabout that led into Horseferry Road."

"We're getting there. My superintendent has given me permission to follow this up, CID are aware, they should be waiting for us."

"That's progress."

"My superintendent put in a good word with the detective chief inspector commanding our division's CID."

"It sounds terribly political, darling, the main thing is that you're on the case, again. That seems only just. After all you were the one who discovered the body and did the spade work, they seem a bit lost."

"Thank you, I do think they need some help."

"It's a strange case."

"We could be seeing the whole extent or just the tip of the iceberg. We could be investigating far more murders but these three hold the key. There's definitely a pattern to the modus operandi but why Battersea, Birmingham and Chelsea?"

"What links them all?"

"Precisely their conditions; their locations have no connection, we always look for patterns but I have to admit, we have nothing."

"What was the flat like where this victim was found?"

"No flat, a house in Chelsea; Charles Wood was a successful and wealthy haberdasher, but he lived in Flood Street not Mayfair or Knightsbridge."

"That's very modern of him."

"He was apparently like that, a little bit Bohemian, he had a reputation as a maverick; he had just appointed his secretary as Managing Director, so he was a controversial figure."

"Forward thinking," Jo acknowledged. She had seen how lecturers and other professionals had not taken her seriously because she was a woman; patients of both sexes had asked to see a male doctor, or by connotation a proper doctor.

"Very!"

It was tough being female and having a career, there was cynicism from males and jealously from females.

"He sounds progressive," she added.

"Exactly, his company had just gone public and the shareholders were up in arms when he appointed her. He said she knew the business inside out but it didn't placate everyone, I'm afraid," I concluded, looking at her profile as she concentrated on steering the beautiful car, it was a heady experience being driven by such an angel.

"You can please some of the people all of the time, you can please all of the people some of the time, but you can't please all of the people all of the time," she recited.

"As you and Lincoln would have it. A few large shareholders said he would live to regret the decision and it looks as if in fact they were right. He died, committed suicide," I observed.

"How sad."

"What do you think he died of?"

"Of a Tuesday?" she joked, smiling at me before drawing on her cigarette. I wondered when the cutting down on cigarettes would actually materialise, there seemed to be much talk about rationing cigarettes and many more excuses to have that extra one.

"From, doctor," I corrected myself.

"Carbon monoxide poisoning."

"Absolutely right."

"Sorry for my flippancy."

"Don't worry, we use gallows humour in the Force, too."

Chapter Fourteen - The Man in Black

Jo crept through the wood, the mulch of old leaves was slippery but she was wearing her après-ski boots, black rubber boots that covered the ankle. They had a thick sole and good grip. She threaded her way through the tall tries, ducking for the older alders that blocked her path.

Oak, Lime, Beech and Silver Birch populated this area of Wimbledon Common area, as well. Strands of spider's webs stuck to her hair, she ducked to avoid twigs and branches and leaves, but she was making progress, moving as silently as smoke.

In front of her, there was the snap of a branch breaking. She could see the man in black ahead of her. He walked up to a small clearing where there stood three trees, a trinity of oaks surrounded by pyres, a great mass of wood created to look like a wigwam at the base of the trunk, it was built from fallen woodland debris.

Wondering whether he had personally built the pyres, she watched as he poured petrol over the collection of broken branches that had been piled up. He drenched the broken limbs; three trees, drenched in flammable material, three victims.

Waiting until he passed up the path, she walked downhill, knowing that the lake was somewhere close by. She crept through the undergrowth, stepping over logs; loose branches littered the forest floor like dislocated limbs. She could see the water glinting in the weak winter sun. Another strand of cobweb caught in her face and latched on to her blonde hair.

She came out into the sunshine, the lake reflecting the clear blue sky above her. There was a single paving stone, which would act as a landmark and then the rim of the lake.

She walked around the circumference of the lake and headed towards Roehampton and the A3. Then she took a fork to where the Roehampton War Memorial stood.

The original war memorial on the site was badly damaged by bombing during the Second World War.

The new memorial was erected in 1952, sited 200 metres east of Roehampton Church. She marked the spot on her Ordnance Survey Map and returned to the *Jaguar*.

Chapter Fifteen - Wimbledon Woods

I stepped out of the back of a *Wolsey* police car. The darkness around me was absolute and the silence of the wood that lay ahead of me was eerily unsettling. I should be able to hear something.

Maybe Jo was wrong after all, I thought to myself.

I closed the door as quietly as I could and my driver, Sergeant Terence Stephens followed suit. We looked across the bonnet at each other, nodding grimly.

The sails of the windmill creaked in the wind that whistled over the heathland. The sky was a midnight blue curtain but large cumulus clouds obscured the waxing moon. His shoes crunched on the gravel as he walked to the nearside wing of the car, he was thankful to be on the grass.

When, after ten minutes walk, they reached the car park at Wimbledon Common was deserted or so it seemed, as they cleared the windmill they saw three cars; there was a white *Rover 75 P4*, a blue *Vauxhall PA Cresta* and a green *Morris Minor*.

Regan tried the doors; all of them were locked. He could feel the thrill of the chase. His driver was alert, his torch flashed briefly in the night before he hid it in his tunic. Adjusting to the darkness, the two shadows scurried along the apron of the car park, their shoes swishing through the dew filled blades of grass, at all costs; they had to avoid walking over the gravel, now that they were so close to their quarry.

According to Jo's map, the ceremony should be happening nearby, just after the common sloped downwards. It should be somewhere between the car park and the lake. Sure enough as they crested the hill that led down into dip, which led to the lake, driver and Inspector were confronted with an ominous sight of a bizarre site.

Three bonfires burnt around in front of the three trees Jo had seen. The firewood stacked up against the trunks had been piled up five feet away from the trees and built into a funeral pyre.

Three men knelt with their hands tied behind their backs. Their suit jackets were missing, they all wore white work shirts that were lit up by the firelight.

Behind them stood three men, resting their hands on their shoulders. All three were dressed in black and wore full-face balaclavas with two holes for the mouth and a slit for the mouth. All six men were silent; they all seemed to be focused on the burning branches in front of them.

The light from the fires guided the police officers to the spot. They watched their footing as they picked their way through the bracken and fallen tree branches. It was dangerous and time consuming but it looked like they had arrived in time.

Regan tripped twice, his driver slammed into a tree trunk, which broke his fall. As they stumbled out into the clearing, six heads turned to look at them.

"Good evening gentlemen, my name if Detective Inspector Regan," Regan elucidated, "can you tell me what's going on here, then?"

No one spoke, Regan realised why the men in business suits would not talk; they had been gagged using silk scarves.

All of the men moaned and groaned desperate to speak, to warn them; their pantomime act lasted a few minutes until one of the men, his face hidden by a balaclava, spoke.

"Good evening, Inspector Regan," he exclaimed, it was a jovial greeting. "I think those three kneeling in their suit trousers are trying to warn you that your trousers are about to get a bit muddy."

The fire gleam lit up the side of Regan's face and a smile was playing on his lips. Bray's face was all leaping shadows, making him seem even more macabre.

"Anthony Bray, I would recognise that voice anywhere. I saw your Rover but I wasn't sure it was you until I saw the number plate, AB 435. This is all a bit melodramatic for an upstanding accountant. Some form of Masonic ritual is it?"

"Your clever cop, Regan, but I would never associate myself with the Masons, they do far too much good for society."

"I should have known, then."

"Of course you should. An old asset stripper like me has no affinity, not even the Rotary Club, of which I assume you are a member."

"Very funny, saw why don't you tell me why we're all here?"

"A ritual execution, if you must know."

"And what have these three victims done to deserve Bray justice?"

"Oh it's not what they have done," Bray replied, keeping his hand firmly on the shoulder, "it's what they were going to do."

"Well, you can let them go, now, can't you?"

"On the contrary you and your sergeant are going to join the party. That's why I led your doctor friend here, so you would swallow the bait."

"So this is a trap?" he scoffed.

The smile on Bray's face was lit by the firelight; Regan knew that smirk would be wiped off his face as soon as the other officers arrived. They should be arriving at any moment.

"I am afraid it is you who are under arrest and you who will be imprisoned," Bray declared arrogantly.

Regan could not believe Bray's gall.

Chapter Sixteen – The Other Party - Jupiter, the Bringer of Jollity

Ray Charles had just finished singing *Let's Go Get Stoned* and a record sent from Jamaica landed on the revolving record turntable, '*Yellow Bird, yellow bird, up high...*"

The only other furniture in the room was an ornate walnut drinks cabinet, from France, in the *Empire* Style, the record player and a small bureau in which stood the black Bakelite telephone. The striped wallpaper was in the regency style matching the dark red carpet that did not show up spilt drink stains. The French windows and skirting board were cream.

The door of the dining room closed blocking out the sound and leaving behind the party. Elegant couples were draped in various states of dishabille on the Berger Suite,

A Polish and Irish doctor had taken one of the two tub chairs, three couples lay back on the sofa and it was difficult to decide who they were, and each of the chairs were occupied, one by a doctor from Ireland and his wife who was a nurse, the other by a dentist and his English wife. The thick cushions and double cane cosseted the exhausted couples, they had been drinking and dancing solidly for three hours.

Outside in the hall

"Another, brandy Alexander Trevor?" George asked.

"Not for me, thank you George."

"Madge, would you like another dinky-donk?"

"Darling, I'm fine, sorry the Browns are very boring. Sadly, we need to leave, Trevor has a dull business meeting tomorrow."

"Darling?" called George, "The Browns are off."

"I'll get your coats, darling."

"Where are they?" Madge asked, opening the cupboard door, rifling through the coats that were hung up on hooks and hangers. Trevor looked sober; he had only had a few brandies. He was going to help Madge, then thought better of it and turned to thank his hosts.

"Right, Jo and George, thanks you for a lovely meal and a super party, we must go to the Alexandria, again."

"The only pub in London with a secret source of beef."

"And delicious it was, too."

Suddenly they heard a crash and a slight scream. Sticking out of the cupboard door was a pair of legs attached to high heels and a prone woman lay under a pile of coats.

"Jo, Jo, I've fallen down the lift shaft."

"Madge, do get up," Trevor insisted, leaning into the coat cupboard to help her to her feet.

"Jo, is that you? I can't hear you down here, I'm in the lift shaft," she complained.

"You can't hear because you've taken all the coats with you," Trevor explained patiently, stripping the coats from her body so he could find her arms and so she could see where she was.

They all laughed, Trevor helped Madge to her feet but as he did so his waistcoat button became entangled in her long blonde hair. Poor Madge was left bending over as Trevor tried to undo and shrug off his waistcoat without pulling her hair. When Trevor had released Madge, George escorted her to the stairs and encouraged her to sit on the third step.

"Wait there, while you get your breath back," George suggested, turning around to see that Trevor had disappeared into the cupboard but at least his legs were not sticking out into the hall, so he appeared to be still upright.

Trevor's disembodied voice came from inside the cupboard, "I've found them; I don't know why you don't let me look for you, especially when you're sozzled."

There was a loud bang at the door and all four looked around. Jo opened the inner front door twisting the small brass handle; the double doors beyond had two locks to secure the door and two bolts that could be rammed home if necessary.

"Who is it?" Jo asked, it was far too late for anyone to call; it was almost midnight.

"Police, Inspector Regan has sent me to collect you."

"One moment officer," she replied.

Madge had been helped to her feet by Trevor and George was helping them to salvage their coats. They all looked at her with mounting concern.

Chapter Seventeen - Climbing the Wall

Jo struggled to release the bonds, she knew she was tied up with her hands behind her back and she knew her face and legs were bruised. They had taken away her coat; she wore a green silk blouse and a beige camel hair and wool skirt from *Jaeger*, tan stockings meant that she was warm but that was the only comfort she had.

"Jo are you okay?" asked a gravelly voice.

She had been expecting to hear George's voice if any one's.

"Regan, is that you?"

"I'm afraid so," he replied guiltily.

"What are you doing here?"

"I'm afraid I owe you an explanation."

"It's not like you to be afraid, I take it something serious has happened for you to be afraid twice in two sentences."

He snorted dismissively.

"It's worse than that, suffice to say that I went to your rendezvous and the officers I had asked to be at the site never materialised, it was like being a charlatan at a séance. Any way my sergeant put up a valiant fight but he was overpowered and knocked unconscious."

"That's terrible," Jo sympathised. "I wondered why you sent a car for me."

"I didn't," he complained.

"I know that, now!"

"So that's why you're here."

"You're the detective."

"Sorry, I fouled up."

"It's not your fault. It wouldn't surprise me if Bray doesn't have contacts all over the force."

"You've met him, then," Regan asked.

"I met him at a fund raising ball," she confessed, "he was threatening my family and I think he was there in Birmingham when I was drugged, he was there or he organised it."

"You should have told me."

"I had no chance to, do you think he is behind all this?"

"I know enough about him to suppose so."

"When I met him that night, I didn't like him one bit, he was sinister," she admitted.

"I think he must have got to one of my men, I had asked for one of my detective constables to organise a police raid on the common, the men never showed up, Bray must have stopped him from passing the message on somehow."

"He's got us both in the palm of his hand."

"Are you religious Doctor   Murphy?" he wondered.

"Yes, why?"

"Better start praying now, then."

"We will get out of this alive."

"It depends on two things."

"What's that?"

"Firstly, if your prayers are good enough and secondly, if anyone in listening."

Chapter Eighteen - Climbing Croagh Patrick

While Jo passed out with the pain, she dreamt. She was taken back to the days when she had walked barefoot up a mountain. As her body dealt with the physical pain, her mind to her back to the last time she had truly suffered one Lent in 1941. Jo placed one bare foot after the other, feeling the shale lacerate her soles; she was climbing Croagh Patrick as part of her Lenten penance; she was joined by thousands of people, but George was not there, they had not met; yet he was able to see the majestic mountain from the fields at Mile Hill House.

Croagh Patrick is situated near the town of Westport in County Mayo, Ireland. The main pilgrimage route originates in the village of Murrisk. It is 2,500 feet above sea level, no special climbing equipment is needed, you can walk up in two hours and down in one and a half hours, if you are wearing stout boots.

There was an Irish expression: All you need is food in your belly, a roof over your head and a stout pair of boots.

Without boots you are lost. As part of their Lenten penance a group of students had come across on the train to Galway and would join other pilgrims in the annual walk up the hill.

They took the coach from Galway to Westport and then on to Murrisk.

From there, they walked to the base of the mountain, where they removed their shoes and wool socks. Most of the people were in corduroy or wool trousers but Jo was dressed in jodhpurs and a white silk shirt that glimmered like mother-of-pearl.

It was 1941 and Jo was nineteen-years-old. She had not known so much pain, he feet, after the first few steps had felt crushed by her body above them, it was infinitely worse than walking barefoot on a shale beach or a tarmac road.

The shards of flint and slivers of stone cut into the flesh of her sole; she offered the pain up to God for the health of her soul.

He had suffered on the cross and on his climb to Calvary, she would suffer on her climb, too, sharing his pain, 'no cross; no crown', 'there are no gains without pains'. The irony of the clichés was not lost on her.

No Cross, No Crown was also a book written by William Penn, the founder of Pennsylvania while imprisoned in the Tower of London, Jo had found his Puritan approach unsettling, she adored beautiful things; he eschewed them.

She did not like reference to pain and gain either, she knew the phrase had been crafted by Benjamin Franklin, in his persona of Poor Richard to illustrate the axiom: God helps those who help themselves. Indeed, she knew the quote off by heart: '*Industry need not wish,* as Poor Richard says, *and he that lives upon hope will die fasting. There are no gains, without pains.*'

There was only one path up and that was like a dried up river bed, full of smooth stones, pumice pebbles and rough rocks all of which were difficult to walk on but the centuries of landfall and landslide, rainfall and mudslide had brought the sharp stones and sharp flints and sharp shards with them and where they subsided was where the walkers stepped.

The narrow path way was bounded by a muddy strip of grass, you could circumvent the path but only with difficulty and no one had dared do it; the quagmire you would end up in would be impossible to escape. The path spread out half way up and the stones were rumoured to be kinder to feet at that point.

Half way up the mountain was where the priest's hut was located. As Jo passed the hut, she distinctly smelt bacon frying, Lent was a time of abstinence and meat of any kind was forbidden throughout the forty days before Easter Sunday. Perhaps, she mused, it was just the bacon fat they were using to cook with that provided the strong aroma, but it made her wonder after all.

Easter was on April 13th that year and the British we fighting to take back Tobruk, The Desert Rats fighting the Afrika Korps under Rommel; Monty was doing well according to the radio reports from the *BBC*. Jo on the other hand was having a battle of her own that day, 10th April, the day before Maundy Thursday. It was a battle of will and determination, fighting the pain in her bare feet, the cold of the mountain and the fasting, which led to hunger gnawing at her stomach.

She dreamt while her body tried to deal with the pain of being bound and the cold. Her whole body was numb, she imagined dying of starvation or hypothermia. Sleep came slowly; she let her mind drift, accepting the stiff arms and legs, the pin and needles and the joints that ached. Inactivity and the inability to move, or get comfortable, nettled but there was little she could do being bound hand and foot.

Chapter Nineteen – The Air Raid Shelter

"Jo, Jo," I called in the darkness.

"Regan, is that you?" she asked.

"How are you feeling?" I replied, my heart skipping a beat.

"Terrible, how about you?"

"I've felt better," I joked.

"Where are we?"

"I think we're in the deep shelters on Wimbledon Common."

"They weren't on the map," I explained.

"Most of them have been filled in; there was only one that I saw still in tact. None of them were on the map, they were designed for councillors during the war when the V2s started to come over."

"So no one will find us here, will they?"

"We'll have to try and get out," I suggested, trying to keep the lack of hope out of my voice.

"What if they have sealed the door?"

"They wanted us dead."

"Dead and undiscovered."

"We can't be stuck."

"It's like an Edgar Allen Poe story, I've always hated the thought of being buried alive."

"Don't think like that."

"Well, that's what's happened isn't it?" Jo argued.

"There's bound to be some other way out."

"I like your wishful thinking but we have to get ourselves untied first of all, don't we?"

"I've got an idea for that," I insisted.

"Really?"

"Trust me!"

"You're meant to trust me, I'm a doctor."

We both laughed heartily, it broke the tension. Listening to each other's breathing, we fell once more into a fitful and dream-filled sleep. When we awoke, she spoke first.

"Are you awake Dick?" she asked.

"Yes, are you okay?" I asked.

"I love a man who answers a question with a question," she quipped.

"I'm awake and alert."

"Good."

"How are you?"

"Dying for a fag, preferably a *Senior Service* but I'll accept a Player's, the use of my hands would be wonderful and the removal of all my pain through a morphine drip would be bliss. What about you?"

"I'm cold, cramped, my back aches, I'm starving and thirsty, I could murder a pint and a pork pie or a ham sandwich, I feel frustrated that Bray is not be where I am now and I have a splitting headache and yes, I wouldn't mind a fag of any description at this time."

"Why do they hate women so much?"

"Fear!"

"Fear, of us, we have to fear you?"

"How so?"

"Come on, you cannot be so naive, or maybe you are decent man and these men are far from that."

"I like to think so," I admitted.

"You must be the only one!" she snorted.

"What about George?"

"He loved my car first, my wealth second and me last."

"Surely, not?"

"I always said we should have just been friends, he wanted to marry me, I said to him 'why spoil a wonderful relationship?'"

"You're happy, now?" I asked, wishing she would say no.

"Of course, darling, but I wanted to be a vet and have twelve daughters, life hasn't worked out quite the way I planned."

"Twelve daughters?" I gasped in awe.

"Yes, to take over the world," she joked, "boys are so beastly."

"Some," I argued.

"All of them, I met my share at medical college. We had to be wily, Jo McCann and I."

"In what way?"

"All the boys pressed forward when the consultant was examining a patient, Jo and I giggled at the back and talked loudly, after all we were too far away to hear his pearls of wisdom. Of course he would hear us and invite us to the patient's bedside, using the patronising epithet, Doctor, asking us for our prognosis."

"A wily way of getting to the front from the back."

"Precisely, the boys were not going to allow us at the front despite the fact that we were first there. They merely crowded us out so we had to get ourselves back to our rightful place."

"Quite right, too."

"And the police force allows women equal rights?" she asked.

"You must remember the case of Ethel Bush," I persisted.

"Remind me," she insisted.

"In 1955, several women were attacked on Fairfield Path, in Croydon. Sergeant Bush volunteered to act as a decoy along with many of her colleagues. The assailant had seriously injured *WPC* Kathleen Parrott in March, and on 23rd of April, he approached Bush from behind and hit her over the head, making a wound that required eleven stitches Bush held on to her attacker's coat and tried to hold him, but fell resulting in his escape. When the attacker was eventually caught, Bush was able to identify the 29-year-old labourer. In response to her actions, she received the *George Medal* for bravery. "

"Impressive, I remember the case, now, I would like to meet her."

"If we ever get out, I'll arrange it for you," I promised, not holding out much hope for us both.

"Promises, promises," she teased.

We spoke no more but dozed through our pain.

Chapter - Twenty

The Cobbler's Children Are The Least Well Shod.

Jo took herself off to a better place, a better time, but a more unsettling situation.

The Northside of Dublin was a den of iniquity and the centre of poverty. Jo was feeling nervous as she walked towards the tenement houses.

She passed the notorious Henrietta Street, once a wealthy enclave, now tenement buildings crammed with residents; at one stage, before the First World War, over eight hundred people had been living in fifteen houses.

Jo's best friend Joanna McCann had arranged to meet her at the end of the street. They had joined a Saint Vincent de Paul drive to help the poor. They had been allocated a family each. Together they walked down the street, chatting happily until the reached the door of number 12, apostolic number, in which they both took comfort.

They chatted amicably with the mother of seven children, all barefoot and thin, but not under nourished.

As they left, Jo slipped a note onto the mantelpiece, fastening it in place with a candleholder, which was the only ornamental piece in the house. Their next call was Joanna's family and it was her turn to leave a five-shilling note. The next week they returned and they mother explained that the husband had taken the money and spent it down the pub. Jo asked her what she needed.

"Shoes for the children, would be grand," she replied.

"Shoes you will have, shall we start with the eldest, what size is she?"

"She's never had shoes but she'll be ten next week."

Jo had seen children walking barefoot when she lived in the East End.

"I have a tape measure in my bag," remembered Jo, "I'll measure her foot and the shoe shop will do the rest."

Arriving the next week with some smart blue sandals, Jo was thrilled when the daughter loved them.

It was a good feeling to help others especially the poor of Dublin, they lived a hard life and anything she could do to ease their suffering was worthwhile.

The following week, she went back to visit their mother, passing by a pawnshop in the high street, she noticed a pair of the same sandals.

Shaking her head at the strange coincidence, she walked on.

At the house she met, the girl, barefoot again.

"What happened to your lovely shoes?" she asked.

"Pa took them to the pawnbrokers to get money for the pub."

Jo's heart sank.

Chapter – Twenty One – George Goes into Action

George rushed out to the street just as the *Jaguar* pulled up to the pavement.

"We're off to collect Regan from the station," George told his driver.

"Clapham Junction?"

"No, *Lavender Hill Police Station*," George replied.

"I'll put my foot down, then."

They pulled out onto Wakehurst Road turned into West Side and shot along the small stretch of road to the junction where the little side road met the South Circular Road, the one way system was name the race track, and the Jaguar was the best car to perform on it. A heavy lorry was coming towards the crossing but they managed to slip into the road just before him ad he has to break for the bend.

Racing from one zebra crossing to the next they scooted around the West Side and merged with a car that was tootling along the North Side. They braked to let it pass before slipping into the left hand lane and turning into Elspeth Road. At the lights, they turned left into Lavender Hill and right into Kathleen Road where they parked.

It had taken them six minutes to get there. Within ten, they were at the sergeant's desk. George was determined to find out what had happened to Jo and he felt sure Regan would know. Little did he know that Regan and Jo were together in the Air Raid shelter and no one knew where they were being held captive.

A dog walker would discover the officer with Regan in time but he would have no idea where the two prisoners were or how long Bray would let them survive. Eventually, he would have to dispose of them.

"Sergeant, I think we might be able to find Inspector Regan," George announced.

"Indeed, Mr.?" he began.

"Fitzpatrick, I'm Doctor Murphy's husband."

"I beg your pardon, of course, you must be very worried."

"I was until I spotted a note left by my wife: unleash the dogs of war," he explained, handing over the note Jo had left on her walnut veneer dressing bureau.

'Dearest Darling George,

Regan has asked me to Wimbledon common, there is a copy of the map where we located the criminals. If I am not back by the morning, unleash the dogs of war. Love as ever Jo.'

"I understand the quote sir, cry havoc and release the dogs of war, I am a fan of Shakespeare's sonnets but I fail to make the connection between that and the predicament of Doctor Murphy and Inspector Regan."

"'The dogs of war' are Remus and Ching, my secretary's dog and my wife's dog."

"Well that is clearer, sir, I thought I was in danger of losing my mind. I'll have the dog section sent to the same location. I take it you have something for them to sniff, or they can follow the little dogs, where are they?"

"I have a Jo's scarf and I have the dogs in the car, yapping and waiting."

"I'll make the call to the sniffer section."

Have you found out what happened to Regan last night? He didn't arrive to collect my wife."

"There's where I can help you, the officer who approached Doctor Murphy to accompany him was not meant to involve her at all. In fact, he was meant to arrange for some officers to surround the area, they were all standing by but they never got the call."

"So, was the policeman who called to our house a bona fide policeman or an imposter?" asked George, furrowing his high forehead.

"As far as we can tell, it was an officer from Regan's section; we had a phone call from his wife shortly after one in the morning saying, he had arrived in a flashy sports car and packed a bag and left, she wanted to speak to the Inspector about it all."

"So he was in cahoots with the kidnappers."

"If the Doctor and the Inspector were kidnapped."

"You don't mean they were murdered?"

"You have to prepare yourself for the possibility. I am afraid Doctor."

"Yes, call me George, please. I refuse to think the worst until we have exhausted every avenue."

"Same here, I admire Regan immensely and he has been very good to me."

"Let's find him, then."

"The inspector's a meticulous man and his report was on his desk along with the action he was to undertake. When I came on duty I pieced everything together and sent a squad car to Wimbledon, they reported back from the police telephone box at Wimbledon Village."

"What did they say?"

"There was no sign of any car except a police car, the very same vehicle Inspector Regan had signed out last night."

"That's very reassuring."

Chapter Twenty-Two – Ching.

Ching was a white Sealyham, a Welsh terrier, which was originally bred to hunt otters, foxes, and badgers. Remus was a black toy poodle, poodles had proved to be an intelligent dog breed second only to the Border collie. Both were trained hunters and George had thoughtfully brought along one of Jo's scarves scented with the perfume she had worn that night, *Ode* by *Guerlain*.

Ching was as white a snow, had long, broad, powerful head was pointed down, his dark, deep-set eyes scanned the grass ahead, he looked up, practically drowning in the long grass, his legs were so short, his well-muscled body straining at the leash. His ears were folded level with the top of the head and the forward edge lay close to the cheek. His tail was upright and resembled an old-fashioned shaving brush. He was on the scent and ready to go. Remus was wagging his puppy tail and following on, he too was a hunter and they both seemed to be heading in the same direction.

The sergeant was the first person they found, the dogs led them to a dip in the ground and on closer inspection of the mounds piled up around and surrounding the depression in the earth, they spotted the two concrete walls that stood on either side of an iron door that looked like it was rusted shut.

George shoved his shoulder into the door and it creaked open. The poor dazed policeman was lying on his stomach, his hands tied behind his back and his feet bound. His mouth was stuffed with a white cotton handkerchief that was tied in place by another. He tried to speak when they entered but all they heard was a muffled mumbling.

"It's all right," George said, hoping his west coast brogue would reassure him, we've come to get you out, I'm with the police. Tomasz and I will untie you and we'll get you to hospital in no time."

The baying of hounds alerted them to the fact that the bloodhounds from the dog section had arrived.

Tomasz and George quickly untied the sergeant, Tomasz untying the Gordian knot at the policeman's feet and George the cutting through the thick rope with a scalpel that was disguised as a fountain pen, which he removed form the inside of his *Chester Barrie* suit and taking off the lid, he sawed through the thick rope. Although the physician cheated the Polish man managed to untie the feet first.

Once free, they helped the sergeant slowly get to his feet.

"Thank you," he sighed.

"What's your name?"

"Terry, Terence Stephens," replied the sergeant.

"Okay Terry, this is Tomasz, I'm George, I'm a doctor, we'll get you out of here and cleaned up, checked over and fed, how does that sound?"

"That sounds bloody marvellous, doctor," he whispered through cracked lips.

"Close your eyes, Terry, we're going outside, we'll lead you; there's a step here, that's it, we'll have you out in no time."

"We've got you, mind the step, lift your left foot, now," Tomasz said encouragingly, "now, the right foot, that's it, nice and steady.

George and Tomasz took an arm each and escorted the dazed sergeant out of the darkness of the bunker and out into the gathering light of dawn.

Terry took two deep breathes of fresh air, the wind whispered through the trees and wisps of morning mist snaked through the Wimbledon woods like lost spirits. Two policemen arrived as the trio emerged into the clearing.

"We'll take it from here, sir," said the elder one.

"You can open your eyes now!" George assured him.

"Thank you doctor," he rasped, his throat parched, it was still difficult to talk.

"Get him some water, and then give him some blankets, I'll come and check him over as soon as I can."

They found Jo and I in the next shelter, a few hundred yards away, thanks, not to Ching and Remus, but thanks to the police dogs that had bounded ahead of the advance party. Experienced and well-trained and cared for, they were expert hunters. Two big, fit and strong bloodhounds strained at their leash scenting the *Ode* by *Guerlain* from Nora's scarf, the scent of jasmine, rose, iris, sandalwood and musk and *Old Spice* from a jumper provided by my wife, Susie.

She had loved the fragrance, the strong notes of sage and cinnamon that she smelt in the morning as I went to work and the pleasant musk and cedar scent that remained at the end of my shift when I returned home. She missed me when I went to work. She would be beside herself, now, especially with the baby to cope with as well.

The dogs had enough to help them locate us, distressed as we were, we hoped we would be saved and Jo's prayers or wishful thinking had worked wonder.

A gathering crowd of policeman crashed through the undergrowth, all in uniform and all wearing wellington boots. There were a dozen officers in all, two sergeants organising them.

Two of them helped Terry towards the ambulance that was parked by the golf club. The other eight followed the two dog handlers. The two sergeants, who were both good friends of mine, pushed open the door to the shelter.

Light flooded into the space, but it was a dull twilight that was almost swallowed up by the darkness. I was closest to the door on an iron bunk bed; Jo was deeper in, sitting on a bentwood chair, her arms tied behind her back.

The dogs came in first, they were overjoyed at having found us; they were wagging their tails and sniffing around excitedly. Their handlers gave them lots of attention. I was glad to see them too but in no fit state to celebrate like them. Hunger had ceased to be a problem by the second day, the body no longer craved food and I was feeling weak like someone recovering from a flu fever.

"I'm here darling," George cried, rushing towards Jo, Remus and Ching barking madly in frenzied happiness. "Tomasz, can you help Regan, please."

"Of course," Tomasz replied, his voice gravelly as he shouted above the noise of the barking.

"You come readily upon the hour!" Jo whispered, her mouth was dry and her voice was cracking.

"Am I glad to see you, the girls have been missing you! I've been desperate with worry, I knew you'd be okay, but I missed you, too."

"Don't worry, I was fine," she mumbled.

"I'll be the judge of that," George insisted, checking her over.

Once he was satisfied, he moved towards me.

"Tomasz how's Regan?" George asked as he strode over to the bunk.

"His hands feels cold, but I've managed to get him untied," he replied, putting his hand on my shoulder.

"Thank you, Tomasz, I'll look after him, can you organise some blankets and bring the ambulance-men down here, please."

"Of course, George," Tomasz answered, leaving George to give Regan a brief examination.

"Sorry about all this trouble, Doctor Fitzpatrick," I mumbled.

"It's George, save your voice, you're both dehydrated, weak from two days without food, no need to apologise, if Jo has faith in you, so do I. Try not to talk, just focus on those clean sheets and warm bed and hot soup waiting for you at hospital. We'll sort everything out, the three of us."

Chapter Twenty three - Bye-bye Bray, Saturn, Bringer of Old Age

"Arthur, it's not like you to be afraid," the voice soothed. Sitting behind a huge desk was Bray's boss, Sebastian Hepher, "a big bully like you acting like a timid victim, I am surprised."

"I don't want to die," replied Bray; his hands on the arms of a red leather chesterfield armchair.

"But what did you say about all those you helped to their early demise? You said you were preserving society, saving the world from anarchy."

"I am."

"Yes but we cannot afford risk of the authorities exposing us."

"Send me to Hong Kong or Africa, I don't mind, just send me away for a few years."

"You need to understand your own rhetoric. Authority is under threat from all areas, the closing of grammar schools, controversial documentaries, the social fabric being worn away by permissive attitudes and nosey newspapers. We need to protect the process and preserve our secrets."

"And I will; I have," Bray protested.

"Up until, now, you know the rules."

"I won't tell, they can't prove it was me; the Tweed brothers did the deeds."

"We gave you a chance; you fell at the final furlong. All you needed to do was get rid of Murphy!"

"I did."

"You were meant to do it discreetly, like all the others."

"She was on to us, I did my best to be subtle."

"Yes, but now the police are investigating the disappearance of Regan and the one policeman that we had convinced to work with us has had to go to ground. Not a great success."

"We all make mistakes."

"Not as many as you have, Bray. Losing the policeman you had in your employ; exposing the Tweeds to investigation, this is not how we operate; allowing Regan and Murphy to get so close. How many times did you try and get rid of her; was it twice? Birmingham and London, both abject failures."

"What are you going to do?"

"That's up to you, you still have your service revolver. I take it; the professor could provide you with a poison to swallow or inject."

"Neither appeal."

"I thought not, that's why we put something in your brandy."

"But I saw you drink from the same decanter."

"A powder at the bottom of your glass."

"Of course, my third mistake."

"Trouble comes not in single spies but in battalions."

"Funnily enough Jo Murphy said the same thing to me at the party."

"Goodbye Arthur, you know we don't tolerate any failure."

"What's going to happen to me?" he asked.

"I should go to bed or at least, sit down, the professor chose a painless exit for you. He choses good old hemlock; death comes in the form of paralysis, your mind will remain awake, but your body will fail to respond and eventually the respiratory system shuts down."

"It won't be painful."

"Of course not and you are in good company. Socrates was executed by hemlock after being condemned to death for impiety. The professor managed make a concentrated form especially for you, he wanted you to go with dignity."

"Just time to write a confession, then," Bray noted.

"I'm afraid not, within a few minutes you will start to perspire and you will lose the ability to move shortly afterwards."

"How long have I got?"

" I would think you will be dead, within the hour."

"Hoist by my own petard!" Bray complained.

"I'll stay with you until you go. Think of me as Saturn, the bringer of old age. I'll keep you company."

"Just making sure I won't write a letter to incriminate you."

"Another brandy?"

"Thank you, one for the road."

"That's the spirit, acceptance is the key, feeling numb yet?"

"I do feel lethargic, but I can lift a glass." he sighed, "I am finding it difficult breathing."

"Not long, now. It's just like dying of old age, slowly you'll drift away into the arms of Morpheus never to awaken again."

"I know, thank you; it's funny, I forgot how callous you could be."

"Life can be bloody, can't it?"

Chapter Twenty-Four - The Train Trip

The sun against the train window warmed her face and she had to close her eyes from its glare. The sky above was so pale it was almost transparent, battalions of clouds massed over the sea flanked by the estuary. The forests coniferous and deciduous, a verdant mass above the train, ferns and brackens lined the tracks. A shiver ran down her spine as they went through the tunnel. Heat and light were extinguished in seconds.

"Did you say your name was Murphy?"

"Jo Murphy."

"You don't sound Irish."

"And you don't sound like an ignorant bigot."

"Point taken, I like a lass who says it how it is. I should be talking with a plum in my mouth too, to be at a shindig like this."

"I like your accent. It's very distinguished"

"Thank you, I say how I see it. It's the Yorkshire way."

"What an elegant way to disguise bad manners."

"I never thought of it as bad manners, telling the truth."

"But surely making people feel uncomfortable is bad manners."

"I don't know about that, the truth's the truth."

"It's the way you tell it, that's what counts," Jo said, smiling at him sweetly.

There was a long silence between them

"I believe you're right," he decided eventually after looking at her closely for a full minute " what brings you up here, lass?"

"You, my dear," she replied.

"What would anyone want with me?"

"You are Sebastian Hepher?"

"Oh, yes, though most people call me heifer, it's a common mistake, not pronouncing my name right."

"And I'm Jo Murphy," she announced confidently.

"Doctor Jo Murphy?" he asked.

"That's correct."

"I've heard a lot about you and your death defying escapades."

"And I've heard about you and not all of it good."

"Why do you court danger?"

"Because I want to see justice done."

"How sweet and reassuring, we have a new generation of women who want a better world."

"What's wrong with that."

"Nothing, nothing at all, but it's a bit difficult to achieve when men are in charge don't you think?"

"We're making progress."

"Yes in some areas, notably medicine. Industry will never change, I'll make sure of that."

"Really, how?"

"You know."

"Yes, I do, thank you."

"But you can't prove anything."

"No, not unless we have someone identify you as the ring leader."

"Shame."

"We seem to be coming into the station; thank you for our chat, I've at least learnt that it is you who was behind all these murders."

"Where do you think you're going?"

"This is Crewe, isn't it, I'm not going all the way to Carlisle, now, I have the information I need, I'll get the train back to London."

"I'm afraid this is the end of the line for you."

Hepher produced a *Webley .455* and pointed it at Jo.

"Really, shooting me in a station in broad daylight and running away, how far do you think you'll get?"

"This gun, the Webley service revolver is among the most powerful revolvers ever produced. I have six shots, ample I should think to execute my getaway."

"I hate the word execute."

"A sensitive soul, I take it."

"What if I were to tell you that there are armed police on this train?"

"I would laugh in your face and call you a lying scoundrel. What sort of fool do you take me for?"

The carriage door slid open.

"An old fool," I announced from the corridor, standing back to allow the armed officer to step in the carriage. "Take the gun with your free hand, take it by the barrel and pop it on the seat beside you and my officer will not have to shoot you."

Jo glanced at me briefly before fixing her eyes on Hepher's, not pleading but challenging. I stayed outside, I did not want to make him nervous, I did not yet know if he had released the safety catch and I was not sure if Hepher would carry out his threat.

"Bugger off copper, I'll shoot her in the heart and save the second bullet for me."

His hand was steady, the gun pointed at Jo's heart; his eyes never left Jo's. I worried that she might be provoking him. She believed he would be less likely to shoot her if he could see her eyes looking into his, trying to connect, a human being to a human being, making her seem less than a target. Had Hepher killed people when he was in the army? I wondered.

"You are already threatening a member of the public with that gun, you have thirty seconds before I allow my officer to shoot you. Lower the gun."

I spoke slowly, allowing him to absorb my words.

There was a loud bang that reverberated around the carriage, Jo curled her feet up and under her, instinctively rolling into a ball. Smoke and cordite curled into the ceiling.

The *Webley* fell to the floor with a thump. Smoke curled from Sergeant Stephens's weapon; the firearms officer's pistol was a semi-automatic *Webley & Scott MP .32*.

Hepher looked stunned at the fact that he had witnessed his gun being shot out of his hand; he held his right wrist as if it were broken. Jo uncurled her long legs and sat up. I sat next to her as the firearms officer trained his gun on Hepher, the barrel was still smoking and the smell of cordite hung in the air. My ears were ringing.

"Well, done sergeant; are you all right doctor?" I asked, putting my hand on her shoulder.

"Fine thank you," she replied as she watched me pick up the revolver from the carriage floor.

"I'll send Mr. Tweed along to identify you officially, Mr Hepher, once we have you securely locked up," I promised.

"Don't think you're won Regan, I have contacts in high places."

"I am sure you do," I sighed, trying desperately to sound calm and collected, one of my best men had been bought by Hepher and his colleagues in crime, I was not as confident as I sounded, nor a sure that Hepher would be locked up for that long.

"Would you like me to look at that hand of yours?" Jo asked.

"It's throbbing not broken," Hepher snapped back ungraciously, shielding his injured harm from Jo's gaze like a spoilt child.

"Good, then you won't object to handcuffs," I noted drily, "Stand up hands behind your back."

I cuffed Hepher and offered the seat between me and Jo to Sergeant Stephens, he had done well, he deserved a sit down. The three of us sat opposite Hepher who seemed anxious all of a sudden, the confidence evaporating as the enormity of his situation began to sink in. If Tweed identified him, he would be convicted as an accessory to murder on five accounts.

"Looks like the end of the line for you," I quipped.

Two officers from Cheshire Constabulary who had searched the carriages until they discovered my uniformed sergeant, Jo and I. Already, my warrant card was attached to my raincoat and I had secured it with a safety pin. As the three of us watched, Hepher, the constables entered the carriage.

"Excuse me and my sergeant for not getting up," I apologised, "it will be too crowded, take a seat gentlemen, there's room next to Mr Hepher, let me introduce you to Doctor Murphy who helped us identify and apprehend Hepher. You mentioned this train has thirty minutes until it leaves for Carlisle, how much time have we left?"

"Twenty minutes, sir."

"Good work, constables, this is our murder suspect, do you mind if my sergeant accompanies you to the station?" I asked.

"Not at all, sir, we have room in the black Mariah, there's three seats in the front and the suspect will be in the back. He'll need to get the handcuffs back anyhow."

"Thank you officer."

"What are you going to do, sir?"

"I will keep Doctor Murphy company on our journey to?" I started before standing up and leaning over to open Hepher's charcoal grey suit. Fishing in the inside pocket, he produced a ticket.

"Where are we off to Mr. Hepher?" Jo asked, smiling.

"Oxenholme," Hepher replied.

"Arthur Ransome renamed it *Strickland Junction* in *Swallows and Amazons* as far as I know," I commented, I was not particularly well read but the novels I did know, I knew plenty about.

"You're a mine of useful information, sir," Sergeant Stephens noted, a touch of irony in his voice, enough for all to suspect but not enough for an accusation of insubordination.

"Thank you sergeant," I breathed, giving him the benefit of the doubt only because of his superb shooting, "you'd best accompany the officers and Mr. Hepher to the station, make a call to the Cumbria Constabulary to let them know we are arriving and get yourself on the next train, I'll leave word with the station master when I get there, hopefully, he'll know somewhere we can stay while we coordinate our next move, better sign out that gun for another few days as well."

"We'll be busy, then, have a safe journey," Sergeant Stephens added, he raised an eyebrow but I ignored it. I was not going to respond to his miming innuendo.

"Yourself, I may forget, your kindness, never," Jo announced.

We all smiled, including Hepher, but his smile was more grudging than all the others.

The officers escorted the handcuffed Hepher to the door, then leading Sergeant Stephens on to the platform, they frogmarched their prisoner out of the station and to the waiting van. Stephens closed the thick heavy metal door that slammed with a reassuring woody thud and scurried after the officers who marched hurriedly to the front of the black Mariah.

Chapter Twenty Five - The Lake District

"So, what's the plan, Inspector?" Jo asked, watching the drops roll down the window of the carriage as the branch line train worked its way through the rain from Carlisle to Oxenholme.

"I'm not sure doctor," I admitted honestly, "I'll pick up some *Kendall Mint Cake* for the wife and children. We'll try and find out where Hepher was booked to stay and put you in a nice place nearby. I'll stay in a room at the hotel where the nest of vipers are sleeping."

"You'll be at risk," she reminded me.

"Oh no, I'll book in under Stephens's name," I assured her.

"You cannot risk being discovered either, check in as Mrs. Fitzpatrick," I warned, "we're close, now, we'll have them soon."

"I admire your confidence, won't it be like finding the needle in a haystack or squeezing a camel through the eye of needle, either way an impossible task?"

"Not so doctor," I asserted confidently and went into Sherlock Holmes mode, "on the contrary, it will be a piece of cake, our arrogant assassins, will use their own names, why bother with aliases so far from the influence of any police force of any size. Secondly, these chaps will only stay in the finest hotels so we merely locate the most expensive hotel in the area."

"The Lake District is a vast area."

"Ah, but our quarry tend to favour proximity to fast transport, they'll want to be close to the station so they can get to Carlisle and then on to their destination in double quick time. It's an old intelligence ploy. Stay close to your escape route. They're all senior executives or Managing Directors; I'll wager, that without exception, they'll all be at the best hotel in Oxenholme."

"Very convincing, Inspector."

"Thank you doctor."

"I would have gone to the most discreet place."

"Yes, but these men are not hiding are they? They are awaiting Hepher and his report."

The train rattled down the track inexorably Oxenholme bound. The rain whipped against the windows and Jo gazed out of the window wondering how she had got to where she was. One night she was pathologist on-call, the next she was helping police with their enquiries, bouncing from Birmingham to Wimbledon to Carlisle and on to Cumbria.

"Where will it all end?" she had asked me.

It was obvious that she missed her three children and George as well as her fairly uncomplicated world and the relative safety it afforded her. Who could blame her for enjoying her existence before becoming embroiled in this caper; this quagmire; this nest of vipers?

She needed to sort out the situation and get back to some semblance of normality. The life of a General Practitioner had its problems but compared to her situation at present, it was a carefree existence.

I thought about my wife and young daughter, she would be too young to miss me, but I missed the missus and the newborn baby. Susie had told me she missed me even before I went away. Duty called. I felt bad about putting Jo in danger and being unable to free us from the bomb shelter but I vowed to do all I could to protect her from now on, no matter what happened.

That was why Sergeant Stephens was armed and why unbeknownst to her, I had signed out a revolver for myself. I convinced myself that I was confident enough to deal with any eventuality but secretly I knew I would feel a lot better when Sergeant Stephens met us. He was to leave word of his arrival at the local police station where I could get a message to him about where we were and what work I needed him to complete.

Both lost in thought, we were lulled by the ostinato of the wheels on the track and by the gentle sway of the speeding train. We would arrive at teatime; we both needed the restorative effect of Assam or Darjeeling.

Chapter Twenty Six – Waterwitch - Neptune, the Mystic

Anton Fox was at the tiller, sitting on the sailing bench, I stood on the steps into the cabin and Jo leant against the boards at the back of the cockpit, her green chiffon scarf saving her hair from blowing around her face.

Both Anton and I wore navy sailing caps, which Anton had brought up from the cabin. There was no mistaking the graceful lines of a *Thirty Square Metre,* its long, lean cigar-shaped hull and lofty, slim-line *Bermudan rig.*

Built by Uffa Fox, in 1937, he had set out to make a yacht with a buoyant hull and succeeding in producing a vessel that was both strong and seaworthy and very quick in the water. Knud Reimers had designed a boat that was forty three foot long and seven foot across the beam, it had a draught of four foot eleven inches and it displaced two and three quarter tons and a sail area of 223 square foot.

Waterwitch was a beauty and she hit eight knots as she keeled over and the wind filled her vast sails.

She was gaining on the other boat, a wooden Wayfarer designed in 1957 by Ian Proctor and manufactured by Small Craft Limited. With a hull and deck made from plywood it was much lighter than the more beautiful *Waterwitch* but she could not compete on speed and sail area with the thirty-square-metre.

John Shallow looked over his shoulder and panic was in his eyes. His escape was being thwarted. He could not believe it. He pulled out his revolver from the webbing belt and holster that he wore over his army surplus serge trousers and serge shirt.

"Sergeant Stephens, put that bucket down and come up on deck, it looks like we're going to be shot at," I shouted.

"Coming, sir, there's not much left to bing up now," he groaned through the hatch that led from the cockpit to the cabin.

"Just make sure you bring your gun, I want that boat sunk before our friend gets a shot off," I continued.

"Easier said than done," complained Stephens.

"We know you like a challenge, get up here double quick. Jo, Anton, both of you get down," I ordered.

Stephens stumbled up the stairs, holding the revolver down by his side, his fingers free of the trigger; there was no round in the chamber and five shells still to be fired if he could hold down the contents of his stomach long enough to discharge the weapon.

There was a tremendous bang that echoed around the lake and all four on deck flinched automatically, the steel mast rang like a church bell as a round embedded itself in the middle of the main mast.

"No one shoots at Waterwitch," Anton complained and turned around to rummage in the cockpit cabinets.

Moments later, he emerged with a flare gun. Shallow was satisfied that the warning shot had produced the desired effect and returned to steering his craft.

Meanwhile, Anton levelled the flare gun at the disappearing boat.

"Are you mad?" I cried.

"Perhaps in the American sense of the word," Anton replied, levelling the pistol at the horizon, tilting it slightly up and pulling the trigger.

The flare coursed through the air, hurtling above the water.
It struck home, hitting the snail, ripping into it, snagging in the torn folds, it ignited the cloth at the same time. The fire spread through the canvas at an alarming rate, eating up the materials and the wind whipped the ashes around Shallow's head.

The boat lost its momentum and drifted, now its propulsion was broken. Waterwitch swept across the water, hauled in tight and sailing herself practically, she was so tightly trimmed.

Anton still kept one hand on the tiller.

"Hold this," he ordered.

Regan held the tiller as still as he could while Anton searched for another flare.

Shallow was turning to shoot at the boat but by now Stephens had moved along the cabin roof and was sitting on the bow, using the bow frame at the front of the boat to steady his arms. Using his right hand, leaning on the bowsprit, he loosed off a round. The explosion sent Shallow sprawling onto the deck of his vulnerable dinghy.

He knew the chances of someone hitting him were slim even though his boat was a sitting duck now; the policeman would have to be lucky to get off an accurate shot when moving at such speed. However, he only had to be lucky once. The boat was running smoothly, there was no buffeting from the waves on such a calm day so the hunters had more than luck on their side, they had the elements helping. Shallow, raised his gun. Anton fired another flare and Stephens loosed off another shot.

Chapter Twenty Seven

"Super shooting Stephens," I announced, lifting a glass of whiskey as we sat in the Saloon Bar of *The Commodore Inn* at Grange Over Sands.

"Excellent effort," Jo agreed.

"I thought Anton's shooting was pretty impressive," Sergeant Stephens replied.

"Thank you," Anton inclined his head in acknowledgement, "but hitting the target at that range from where you were sitting is nothing short of miraculous; as the French say: *chapeau*; I take my hat off to you."

"The mutual appreciation society's annual gathering will be called to order," I quipped, lifting my whiskey glass.

I am partial to a bit of whiskey and soda before dinner, the Commodore had an especially well thought of dining room but an even friendlier and cosy bar. We were all having an aperitif; Jo had a brandy and soda, Stephens was swigging form a pewter jug with pale ale in it and Anton, international set show-off that he was drank Carlsberg.

It was the thin end of the wedge, buying a Swedish boat, drinking Danish beer and driving us all here in his SAAB. Anton was a Swiss name not Scandinavian but you would have thought our friend was from Stockholm and his name was Edvard by the way he behaved.

His 1957 Saab 93 was parked outside, it was *Scandia Snow* or some such white paint effect people gawped at the trademark trapezoidal radiator grill and the beetle-like lines, it looked live a VW that had been sat on and its headlights moved closer together. We were all a bit rattled from the shoot-out and from chugging down here in Anton's cramped three-cylinder car. At least the seats were fairly comfortable.

"Three down, three to go, cheers," I toasted, smiling first at Jo and then at the rest of the supporters' club.

All of us appreciated spending time in the presence of charm and beauty.

The mood in the bar was good. Bray had been found dead, CID had informed me, we had Hepher in custody and Shallow was in the local nick awaiting a pick up and transfer back to London to answer questions from my CID colleagues. It seemed like we had finished off the trio's rule of terror.

No longer would that unholy trinity use their bullying tactics to threaten, maim and kill. One of the Tweed twins had been taken care of and, without a paymaster; the other would fade into the background.

I was sure he would crawl out of the woodwork at some later stage, working for someone else.

"Confusion to our enemies," Jo added, raising her glass.

"Skol," Anton said, I was convinced that he wished that he had been born a Scandinavian.

His blue eyes and blond hair certainly helped him to look like someone from an Ingmar Bergman movie, *The Seventh Sea* or *Wild Strawberries*. I had read about them both, seen a trailer at a cinema; seen a few stills in the foyer. Susie loves to go to the cinema. She goes to see that sort of film with a friend of hers, the mother in law comes over and she goes off to the '*flicks*'.

"Cheers," echoed Stephens, the hero of the hour.

Stephens was a good copper; he was a superb sergeant and I would miss him when he was promoted. His keen eye and loyalty would be hard to replace. Shooting the gun out of Hepher's hand was a masterstroke and may have saved Jo's life; Hepher might well have pulled the trigger. His shooting on the lake was another stroke of genius.

He had shot twice, holing the boat with each shot and putting the fear of god into its captain. Poor old Shallow, as he sank, he was still trying to put out the flames that had engulfed his sails. Anton's second flare had snagged in the foresail and that had caught fire, too. Canvas burns remarkably quickly. Shallow did not have a chance to have fire his gun again, he had to swim and the fool had no life jacket. Anton had insisted we all wear one.

At the bottom of the lake, there was a weapon, a boat and charred sails. Shallow was left treading water. Anton bought Waterwitch alongside and I fished the slippery customer out of the water.

Somehow, Anton got the boat close enough for me to spear his jacket with a boathook and we towed him to the jetty. He did not struggle, the water was freezing and we were saving him from swimming and hypothermia. All he wanted was to be warm and dry. A nine, nine, nine call brought an ambulance and a blanket as well as the local police who provided him with a cold cell for him to reflect on his bad luck.

Jo had tracked him down, he had not expected that; she had challenged him, he had not expected that; she had pressed Anton into making chase as he made his escape in his own boat; he had not expected that.

We would all sleep better in our beds, knowing this nest of vipers had been destroyed.

Jo was on sparkling form; she was telling funny stories, which were close to the knuckle, 'medical' jokes, she called them. The other two went puce with laughter. I could not possibly repeat them in front of my grandson so you will have to imagine what she said.

Suffice to say that we had a wonderful evening, there were several more drinks and we had some freshwater fish, bream I seem to remember. I do remember Jo ordered a bottle of *Pouilly Fume* to go with it, which was generous and it was delicious. It came from the Loire and I had never tasted such a flinty dry wine, it was an education, my knowledge of wine at that time was minute. We all drank beer or whiskey in South Norwood.

Stephens drank far too much but since he had been the hero of the hour, we all turned a blind eye. It turned out his wife was Spanish and his in-laws had educated him in the delights of wine and he was means tot be used to it. He should have known better but pulling the trigger twice in one day affects a man.

Today he would have counselling after discharging his weapon, back then, he was expected to just get on with it. I think he had killed a few people during the war and firing the gun brought that all back to him. We never ever talked about the war but most sergeants in those days who had firearms licences had seen active service in the Second World War.

If they were around, now, they would be writing *Blogs* about the trauma of war and suing the government for all sorts. We were shattered by the experience and the meal did much to lift our spirits. Stumbling to our rooms exhausted but satiated we all slept like logs, slightly sozzled logs, more Christmas pudding than Yule log.

The Saab was quite quick for a motor with only three cylinders, Anton, I had later ascertained, was a biker as well as sailor and he drove like he was on his flipping bike, making bends in the lanes more like chicanes. It was like a horizontal roller coaster,

Stephens sat in the front gripping hold of his seat and Jo and I were thrown around in the back. She laughed as she slipped on the leather seat and slammed into me, I kept apologising every time I slid over on a corner of the opposite line. I did not want to crush her so I held on to the red leather strap that hung from the ceiling.

Jo was dressed for flying, a pair of baby blue Capri pants and a cream blouse topped off with an United States of America Air Force, brown leather jacket. If she had been a drink, she would have been poured into a glass without saying when.

 Every piece of material clung to her body; the Capri pants looked like they had been sprayed on to her body and her jacket looked like it had been tailored to fit her like a glove. It certainly showed off her curves. I dismissed all these thoughts, I was married and she was married. I was allowed to look and I was certainly able to admire her. She had a wonderful body, tall, lithe and strong. Jo was a slender Boudicca with curves in all the right places.

We were heading for White Cross Bay Airfield on the Allthwaite Road, after a few miles we turned on to the Cartmel Road; Sergeant Stephens was going on to Cark Station to start his journey to meet with our Scottish colleagues.

Anton had graciously agreed to be chauffeur and I think he was expecting to have Jo next to him on the journey. I would not have been surprised if his hand had slipped off the gear lever and on to Jo's thigh if she had.

Whether Jo was being wise or just kind to Stephens, she insisted on sitting in the back with me. Maybe she felt I was the safest of the three of us. I had noticed Stephens' lustful looks as he got more pie-eyed last night and I know Jo would have picked up on that.

Anton was the only unknown quantity, but he was also the only single man amongst us, so it was only Jo's wedding ring that might prevent him from making a move on her.

There was just too much testosterone in one confined place and me being thrust against Jo's thighs and breathing in her Guerlain perfume did not help with my moral fortitude. I had to fight hard to restrain the animal urge to dive on her neck and kiss her nape.

Instead, I stared out of the window, hanging onto the strap and trying to prevent my thighs from sliding over to Jo's side of the seats. Ignoring Jo's giggles when he thighs slid over on to my side and brushed against me.

She thought it was fun; I thought it was torture. Stephens was silent, being hung-over and Anton was enjoying setting up the *SAAB* for all the bends, braking before the bend and accelerating into the corners. Then opening the engine out on the straight.

I still remember the roar of the engine, he was keeping the revs high and the motor was working hard but I must admit he was a skilful sailor and driver, intuitive and fluid and I admired the nippy car and the man who was getting us to the airfield as fast as was humanly possible.

Cark Airfield was home to what we know today as the *RAF* Mountain Rescue Unit. It arrived there in 1944 from around the corner at *RAF* Millom, seeking out aircraft that had crashed on the lakeland fells. '188 Gliding School' continued to use the airfield until May 1947 when it was sold off; Cark re-opened later for private use, initially by the Lakes Gliding club.

In 1959, there were a few private air clubs and this one had a *Piper* and a *Cessna* for hire; I had never flown before and the idea of a single engine plane made me uneasy. Anton was curious about the engine.

"What type of engine do these planes use?" He asked as we swept through the gates, a phone call from the hotel meant that they were expecting us and the ground crew would have heard the howling SAAB a mile off.

"A six cylinder engine," Jo replied, nonchalantly.

One engine with only a six cylinder engine to get it airborne; I did not like that. I did not like flying just like some people so not like liver but have never tried it. Liver done well is delicious.

The white and red *Cessna 172* had a tricycle landing gear, being a variant of the tail-dragger Cessna 170 with larger elevators and a more angular tailfin. Jo turned me from train-spotter to plane-spotter that day. I looked up all about light aircraft after the caper, suing my local library to find out all I could. I did not know, at that stage, that a *petrol-head* could be into cars and planes.

Our *172* had fixed wheels on the front under the wings and the third wheel under the tail. The only 172 I had known up until then was the double decker that went from Honor Oak Park to Farringdon Station via, New Cross, Elephant and Castle, Waterloo and Aldwych.

At least, the plane looked new. That made me feel slightly less nervous, but not much. I think it was a year or two off the production line. It was American so that guaranteed reliability.

"You three grab a tea while I go over the flight plan and complete the pre-flight checks, it will take some time," she announced as she walked off with the flight supervisor.

After forty-five minutes and two cups of tea, I visited the toilet and when I came back Anton was shaking Jo's hand and trying to kiss her cheek, the cheeky so and so. Jo managed to turn to Stephens and shook his hand so Anton was left pouting at a black and white photo of the airfield in the Second World War.

It was freezing outside, a strong wind coming off the sea, wet and chilled. Climbing into the plane only took us out of the howling wind; it was not much warmer inside. It was quieter and more comfortable once we had struggled into our seats and strapped on the strange seat belts that just went across the lap.

She was dressed for flying; I was dressed for investigating. My beige mackintosh over my grey suit and my brown trilby were my only protection from the elements, a part from gloves and a blue tartan scarf. Then, Jo opened the window I was just about to tell her off and shout at her to shut it when the Flight Supervisor, arrived.

"Everything all right?" he shouted up at the window.

"All okay," Jo replied, smiling down at him and then watching as he made his way to the front of the aircraft clear of the propeller

"Mixture rich, carb heat cold, throttle open a quarter inch," Jo mumbled.

"Contact!" he cried.

"Clear prop!" Jo replied.

I just wanted the blooming window closed, the chill wind was crawling into the cockpit and I did not like it. She turned the ignition to start her up. Nothing happened,

"Give her another try," the supervisor said.

She repeated her mantra about rich, cold inches, turned the ignition and the engine roared into life, shaking the airframe and filling our ears with noise. I felt like a cocktail in a shaker as the plane gyrated around us.

"Chocks away!" Came a disembodied voice and I assumed the supervisor had taken away the wooden blocks that kept the front wheels from rolling and he had headed to the tail of the aircraft.

Finally, Jo closed the window and the wind died down, she moved the throttle forward and we eased towards the runway.

The propeller, which had seemed such a huge feature of the plane when I looked out at as we sat in the plane, while Jo carried out her pre-flight equipment checks, had vanished. It had becoming a blur of high-speed spinning. I really did not notice it at all; it disappeared swallowed up by its own speed. I was amazed.

The vibration reached fever pitch, I was being jostled about and shaken up like a milk shake in a blender. Jo steered with her feet, this plane relied on the pilot pressing the right rudder pedal the skid pivoted to the right, creating more drag on that side of the plane and causing it to turn to the right.

My whole body shook and I tried to look calm and composed. I thought my hat was going to be shrugged off my head so I put one hand on the crown to kept it down.

That was not the only thing I had to keep down that morning, we had fried eggs, bacon and fried bread for breakfast at the hotel. It was a two-fold move. One to get rid of my hang over and two because I knew we would not be eating until late afternoon, a hearty breakfast, which I regretted as we trundled our way to the landing strip. I have both a nervous disposition and a sensitive stomach. It was bad enough trying to recover from the effects of the alcohol, the greasy unctuous breakfast but the trundling over the runway almost proved too much.

Steering a plane on the ground is not easy. There is not enough speed to bring most of the controls into action. To turn left or right, you have to increase speed on one side and decrease it on the other. By dragging one wheel you turn in that direction. While being so much less effective than a steering wheel and wheels that steer, the drag method, also jolted us around much more, too, which did not do any favours to my queasy stomach.

It only gave the pilot some control of the direction the craft was moving while taxiing or beginning the take-off run, before there was enough airflow over the rudder for the rudder to become effective.

"Are you okay, Inspector?" she asked, glancing briefly up from her instruments and the returning to look out of the windscreen. At that point we were rumbling along over divots in the grass and Jo was manoeuvring the craft to the left at the same time.

"Fine, doctor, thank you," I replied, feeling a small amount of reflux travel up my throat.

"Dick, you look a little green about the gills," she teased.

"Just getting used to the steering method over this type of terrain," I bluffed, trying to muster up a smile but giving up when I realised she was intent on getting us airborne and not establishing a rapport with me.

Jo assured me she was familiar with this method of flying and the less common 'differential braking', in which the tail-wheel is a simple, free caster mechanism, like a wheel on some furniture, and the aircraft is steered by applying brakes to one of the main wheels in order to change direction. I failed to realise the difference between both methods no matter how many times she explained it, then and of course subsequently Nowadays, this is usually integrated with the rudder pedals on the craft to allow an easy transition between wheeled and aerodynamic control.

My throat was dry and I wore a fixed grin as we rumbled along the grass towards the runway, which I could not make out, it just looked like when very narrow, very long field with hedges all around. It was noisy in the plane so neither of us spoke. We were strapped in and, I folded my hands in my lap, glad that I was wearing my lined brown leather gloves; coppers always invest in warm gloves, it comes from years of freezing fingers on point duty.

After her left turn, she motored up the airfield and then after an age of rattling and rumbling across the worst terrain in England, she took a sharp right so that she could turn into the wind for take off. The molehills and dips strewn across our path would have made a seasoned pirate feel seasick

There was still dew on the roof of the cabin. I could feel the cold crawling under my coat and trying to sneak into my suit. Miraculously, the seats were not wet but I guessed that Jo had wiped them down when she was completing her pre-flight checks, it would be the type of considerate thing she would do. A scrunched up towel on the floor between us seemed to confirm my suspicions.

Scarcely had I acknowledged its presence when we accelerated sharply. Suddenly, I saw the tight grip Jo's gloved hands had on the throttle as she pushed the plane further and further and faster and faster along the runway. It was then I decided I wanted to walk to London but I was too petrified to move and my mouth so grim set that I could not speak or scream.

Hurtling along the runway was like being next to Jo in the *Rolls* only we were much higher up and the ride was a lot bumpier. Where the Rolls was a vehicle that was all comfort and sumptuous luxury, the plane was sparse, practical, all austerity and simplicity.

My spine tingled and a trickle of cold sweat ran down from my armpits as we hared along the grass at breakneck speed, heading for the hedge. I glanced over at Jo and she wore a look of grim determination.

Then, it happened.

We were airborne, I knew because there was this incredible feeling of weightlessness. I literally felt as light as a feather. We had left the shackles of the earth and we were actually flying.

Looking over at Jo, I noticed her face had relaxed and she was smiling. I was glad one of us was enjoying the experience. I began to relax and trust in her, her abilities and the plane. The initial foreboding was replaced by this amazing feeling of freedom, we had left the confines of the earth and we were soaring above it. There was no more shaking and bumping, we were floating and it was infinitely more preferable than being on the ground. I decided not to worry about the landing that was about two hours and two hundred and forty nautical miles away.

Everything was flying by us, the bare branches of the trees flew by, the green grass of the airfield whizzed past the window and then we were way above the ground and below the clouds but climbing. Flying is an amazing experience; I love it thanks to that day. It's a miracle how bigger and bigger planes take off and land safely, back then only the select few flew.

Being in a light aircraft was sheer bliss. The plane no longer vibrated it quivered in the wind, trembling almost imperceptivity. We were cruising at about 120 miles per hour. I knew the plane could go faster but hurtling above the ground in a small tube made me realise how fast that actually was. It was a strange feeling the speed felt no greater than cruising along the streets of Battersea looking for criminal activity. The noise was slightly more annoying than Sergeant Stephen's profane and inane chatter.

We were buffeted about by the wind at first, a squall coming off the Irish Sea but then Jo climbed a few hundred feet, eased back on the throttle and we settled into a wonderful motion as straight as an arrow at about three hundred feet off the ground. It was amazing, the view was incredible, I do not like heights, never have done but this was different, I wasn't on the sixth floor of a building, I was behind a screen in a seat and I could see fields stretching across the horizon, hedges and roads criss-crossing our path, mirror lakes like shards of broken glass reflected the grey curtain of sky above our heads.

It was blooming cold up there and Jo put on the heater, which was remarkably effective, blowing hot air from the engine into the cabin. Soon we were toasty.

We ventured a conversation, which became a shouting match as we tried to hear each other over the loud thrum of the petrol engine. It lasted long enough for me to compliment her on her flying skills and for her to explain our route.

I left her to look out for landmarks and watch the dials in front of her. We were flying on instruments but she had the pilot habit of checking everything visually just in case the instruments malfunctioned.

Jo was enigmatic, she kept her thoughts to herself but she did share the fact that she had been thinking of her sister, Moira, who had married into the Finucane family. She told me she always thought of Paddy Finucane the air ace when she flew. He had been a great hero of the Second World War.

He had also been one of my sister's crushes during the same war, Juliet was seven years older than me, and my mother had miscarried several times before me.

Juliet knew him as Wing Commander Paddy Finucane, his nickname, he was actually called Brendan Eamonn Fergus Finucane and he was awarded the Distinguished Service Order, DSO and The Distinguished Flying Cross, DFC. He was an RAF pilot who had been credited with five or more enemy aircraft destroyed in dogfights and that made him an ace but he was also the youngest person ever given command of a fighter wing in the history of aerial combat.

Finucane was credited with twenty-eight aerial victories, five probably destroyed, six shared destroyed, one shared probable victory, and eight damaged.

On 15 July 1942, Finucane took off with his flight for a mission over France. His Spitfire was damaged by ground-fire.

Finucane attempted to fly back to England but was forced to ditch into the sea and subsequently vanished. As you know, the name was more recently associated with Brendan Finucane's nephew, the Northern Ireland solicitor, Pat Finucane. During *The Troubles*, he defended both sides in legal cases, winning human rights actions brought against the British government and he was allegedly murdered by Loyalist paramilitaries acting in collusion with the British government intelligence service MI5 in 1989.

Paddy Finucane was a brave and successful pilot and his exploits were widely reported and I think my sister fell in love with the dashing and daring chap. She was only sixteen. There was a five-year gap between the two of us; my mum lost a baby in between.

We spoke about the war briefly, when we landed. I was twenty-seven in 1959, so I was only seven when war broke out and I was ten in forty-two when Finucane was flying about, almost thirteen when it was all over. Jo was ten years older than me; I was born in 1932. Juliet was fourteen when the war broke out, seventeen when Finucane's face was first shown in the newspapers and twenty when she married a Canadian and moved to Lethbridge, Alberta.

Her war was spent in Bromley House in Kilpedder but she did tell me about what happened to her aunt as we travelled in the police car I had arranged to pick us up and take us from the plane to London.

A Close Shave for Jo

White Waltham was one of the oldest and best-known airfields in the country and the largest grass airfield in the country. The airfield is situated just four miles from the A4, the road from Bristol to London. Central London was only thirty-five miles away.

The airfield might have been the largest airfield in England but it looked like a green silk handkerchief, small and slippery. The engine had become a dull drone in the background but we had been lost in our thoughts. I was trying to work out how we could tie up the loose ends of the case and running through the evidence we had so far. Suddenly, I was dying for the toilet and the airfield appeared as we broke through the clouds.

During the flight, I had just been bouncing about in the plane, listening to the loud noise and trying to pretend I was in a car. When we were about to land, I suddenly felt nervous. We were travelling fast, I could see both the altimeter and the speedometer, we were dropping fast and we were aiming for a narrow airstrip. Taking off on grass had been traumatic; landing on grass was going to be worse.

The ground was coming closer and closer, the plane did not seem to be going any slower, although the rate of knots was dropping, according to the dials, our height was diminishing by the second. Ahead of us I could see the wooden hut and four airplanes lined up on the grass beside it.

Jo flew past, dipping her wings, and circled above the airfield, a pocket of wind lifted us up and it was like being on an elevator, my stomach lurched but by now my breakfast had digested and if fear had not distracted me, I might have been hungry. Coming in for her approach, we lurched upward, there were pockets of air all around.

She was an experienced pilot and as we raced towards the ground, she increased the power to push through the air currents and adjusted the trim.

This was the worst part for me and I felt my body stiffen and my hands were clammy. I could feel sweat forming on the brim of my hat.

The wingtips seesawed slightly and then we were sinking like a boat, I could feel us going under. Sinking too fast, as far as I was concerned. Still we continued sinking in the sky, nearing the ground. Rather too rapidly for my liking, the ground came up to meet us and I felt even more nervous, my anxiety stemming from the approach of trees and shrubs which I felt sure we would hit and would flip us over.

Then, the most enormous thump shook the whole plane, making the airframe shudder. We bounced up like a kangaroo and landed more gently, the frame rumbled, before we bounced up again, just a short hop and, then, we made contact with the ground. A mere jump, skip and hop was all it needed for my heart rate to stop soaring to record levels. I felt like Bannister after he had run the four-minute mile. I reckon he was less sweaty and his heart was not trying to jump out of his chest.

The speed at which we hit the ground shook me up, it was my first landing and the speed at which Jo decelerated shook me up even more, I felt like a Café Royal Martini by the time we had reached the apron, thoroughly shaken.

The driver introduced himself and immediately Jo handed her cigarettes out and Anderson acted as if it was Christmas, he had always smoked *R.N.* and had only once or twice come across *Senior Service*, he took one enthusiastically and led us to the car, which was the standard *Wolsey* issue. It was waiting for us outside the aero club hut and as we slid into the backseat, I felt relieved to be back on terra firma and easing into the read leather bench seat of a *Wolsey*. It was warm inside. Anderson had obviously kept the heating on during his trip down from Battersea.

After chatting briefly to the driver, Sergeant James Anderson for the record, we learned he was ex-Royal Navy, convoy protection, we settled back into our seats and started our conversation about the war brought on by Anderson's proud proclamation about his previous profession. He had a good war; he came back, which was a miracle when you were trying to get across the Atlantic with all the U-boats around. Anderson could not keep up with the conversation being in the front, so he concentrated on driving up to old London town. The two-hour flight had felt like eight. So we relaxed into our seats.

That was when she told me about Finucane and her time in the Blitz. I was in Kent when the Blitz came, not a sensible place with hindsight but at that time the bombers were taking their load of bombs to London exclusively. I was out of the firing line, Jo and her family were not.

When the bombs started dropping in England, Jo was still at school, she was on holiday at the outbreak of hostilities in July 1940, when the Battle of Britain was being fought; she was in the East End of London. As long as the Germans targeted the airfields Londoners were safe. She went back to school on the first day of September.

Jo was just eighteen, two years older than Julie. On 4th September the Blitz started when Hitler changed the focus on raids to the civilian population. Jo was to be sent to Liverpool and across the Irish Sea to Dublin and from there she could get a bus to Bromley in Kilpedder. She was sent to spend the night with her aunt at the Cross Keys in E.C.1.

She slept in one of the top rooms and the next day left for Liverpool from Euston. That night the pub that she had been staying in suffered a direct hit.

"What happened?" I asked, "I knew the terror of an air-raid that my mother tried to hide and the jangling of my own nerves.

"My father closed is his pubs and took his men to dig for his sister," she explained.

"Did they find her?" I asked.

"They dug for four days, clearing all the rubble away. The only thing that they found, which belonged to my aunt was her hand. My father recognised the engagement ring. They never found her husband."

"That's terrible," I sighed, feeling myself about to wretch, my imagination can be too vivid sometimes. I can still see that cold pale hand in my dreams sometimes.

"There's more," Jo added, I hoped she did not see my involuntary shudder, if she had she just ploughed on.

"They found the nurse who had taken over my room after I left," she said.

"Where?" I asked.

"In the cellar."

"What happened to her?" I instinctively inquired, once a cop and all that, I immediately regretted it.

"They found her in the corner of the cellar with her hands blown off, she had bled to death through her wrists."

I remained silent, my lips were sealed, I tried to look sympathetic but it was tricky when I had vomit crawling up my throat and into my mouth. I swallowed hard and fixed her gaze. Our eyes communicated our sadness and loss. I shuddered to think that if she had been there one more night she would not be here next to me.

It was then I realised how much I was falling for her. It was corny and unrealistic, I was in love with my Susie but I suppose I was also a little bit in love with Jo, too. That was allowed. I was never going to act on any of my feeling for her. I was quite prepared to love her from afar. It was going to be a story of unrequited love but a love of sorts nonetheless. I was doing nobody any harm. The only damage was the ache in my heart every time I thought of her.

Chapter Twenty Eight - Return to London

We arrived back at eighty-eight at six, in time to see Bubs and the children. George was visiting the Black Lion in Kilburn High Road. I left Jo and was driven back to Penge; I had missed Susie and our baby boy, Kenneth. He was named after Susie's uncle. We both needed rest but there was no rest for the wicked in those days and the righteous needed none. Sergeant Stephens picked me up at eight thirty, I had barely spoken to Susie but I had managed to help settle Ken and finish my high tea. It was a moveable feast. Taking the last morsel of bread and swilling the last of my tea, I heard the doorbell and rushed to answer it. Susie and I knew that it would be him and that it was a call to arms. She shrugged her shoulders. Behind every good copper is an equally long-suffering and supportive wife.

In the car driving to central London, Stephens filled me in.

"Okay sergeant, what's going on, it better be good, I've only just got back from Cumbria," I complained, settling into my seat and buttoning up my mackintosh against the cold.

"I've contacted Jo, were heading to West Side, then we'll move to Wetherby Gardens," explained Stephens.

The Three Musketeers were to see action again, I thought ruefully, not realising at the time that firearms would be used.

"So why Wetherby Gardens?'

"CID has been keeping the top floor flat of number one under surveillance. It's Jenny Strong's *pied de terre* apparently but she has not been there for days."

"So CID should get a warrant to search, surely?"

"That's in the pipeline, but the sergeant contacted me to say that the surviving Tweed twin was seen sitting in a green Mini van in the same street."

"Eagle eyed, sergeant, he did well to spot Tweed," I said, looking over admiringly at Stephens who shot me a brief sideways look and a smile.

"Sergeants do all the work while our detective inspectors get all the credit," he joshed, flipping on the windscreen wipers as the rain came.

There was a crescent moon that kept hiding behind the advancing cumulus clouds, their bellies swollen with rain. It was just a local cloudburst but it did not put either of us in a good mood, Stephens because he had to reduce his speed in the wet, for myself, I had the gloom of many nights, too much time freezing to death on the beat had made me morose.

"So why are they letting us know about it?" I asked, knowing it was not like the boys from CID to share the glory or an arrest with us mere mortals.

"Someone obviously likes your smile, sir," he quipped.

"So we're both in the dark."

"Some things never change."

We were left to our own thoughts as we drove up the hill to Crystal Palace, down the other side to Streatham to join the South Circular Road. Stephens raced from Cavendish Road to the racetrack, took a left into Bowood Road and then left again into Wakehurst, pulling up outside the front door.

Chapter 30 – Wetherby Gardens

i

We collected Jo of course; it was on the way from my home to Wetherby Gardens. We had instructions to meet the CID on the corner. They were in a white Ford.

On our way, we passed an accident on Lavender Hill.

"That reminds me of my first R.T.A.," I exclaimed before explaining needlessly that is stood for road traffic accident.

"When was it?" she asked, she was an expert at getting people to talk.

"It was in fifty-four. It involved a motorcyclist, a car and a truck. After the ambulance had been, I was told to help clear up; I picked up the helmet and the rider's head was still in it," I bragged, it was a good story, though the memory of it made me shudder inside.

I hoped it would shock Jo for some unknown reason; maybe it was a story that made me look tough, tougher than I was, in fact. It might have been due to my failure to protect her at Wimbledon Common that now I wanted to show her how manly I could be..

"How awful, I remember my first craniotomy, we just could not get the baby out and we couldn't perform a Caesar as the baby's head was engaged," she said. "She was a mother of eleven, so there was simply no other choice. We had to save her. I still shiver to think of the decision I had to make but the baby was almost dead already. If I hadn't performed the operation, both of them would have died."

That shut me up.

I realised, then, how similar our lives were, we had to take tough decisions and we had to clear up the mess when things went wrong.

We sat back in the car as Stephens drove us along the rest of Latchmere Road, past Battersea Park Road and onto Battersea Bridge.

We stared out of our windows at the city as it was lit up for the evening.

We were left to our own deep and dark thoughts.

Memories crowded into my mind, I even remember some of them, now, but the rest of the evening is a bit of a blur especially just before I was knocked out. That was why I needed Jo to fill in the details.

I remember us arriving at the building, noticing that there was no car there and leaving Stephens and Jo to look for the Ford around the corner. That was when I must have been hit from behind.

So there we sat in Lyons' Coffee House, our drinks getting cold a Jo reminded of what happened that night in her own words. I had read the report but it skimmed on most of the salient details. I wanted the inside story.

As far as I was aware, I was knocked out and woke up with Stephens standing over my hospital bed. He had taken me down the road and around the corner to St. Stephen's Hospital, a small hospital on Fulham Road; it was less than ten minutes away.

ii

I was looking out for a white or black *Ford Zephyr*, it was a popular choice for the C.I.D, the Anglia was not glamorous or large enough for the big boys. It had been particularly warm and comfortable in the car and leaving those cosy confines was a huge shock. As I shut the door carefully behind me, I felt the damp air and chill wind try to seep into my very bones. Buttoning up my mackintosh, I strolled to the corner. The operator had definitely told Stephens that the rendezvous would be on the corner opposite Wetherby Gardens.

There was no sign of any cars at the corner, there was only one old *Bentley* in the street. I walked to the corner, there was nothing in Bolton Gardens to the south and only a few cars in Collingham Gardens to the north, A *Standard Vanguard* and a *Morris Minor* were parked on one side of the street and a *Rover P4 75* with a single fog lamp in the middle of the grill, the 'Cyclops Rover' and a *Vauxhall Velox* on the other. I had been expecting a Bristol or Aston Martin but I was disappointed. Then, the ran came, spitting pathetic flecks of rain on me and the pavement.

I walked a few yards down to the Boltons and then crossed over retraced my steps but on the opposite side of the road, I looked left as I crossed into Collingham Gardens but there were no vehicles there. My breath came out in clouds and I shuddered with the cold. It was time to get back to the warmth of the car and the smell of Jo's *Guerlain* perfume. I crossed over to the other side of the road and I could hear my leather soled shoes slapping on the wet pavement.

Next, I heard the sound of rubber-soled boots thumping on the wet concrete. As I turned, a cosh hit me in the temple. It felt like I had been hit with a brick. I remember steadying myself against the garden wall. Dazed I looked around at the hedge that marked the gardens, I dimly registered that my assailant had come from there. I staggered forward using the wall of the building for support.

I wondered why he had not come at me again, but as my legs buckled underneath me I knew why. He   knew exactly what he was doing.

I felt weakness wash over me in waves. My head ached. I had to make it to the corner and warn the others, the soul was willing but the flesh was weak. Every step was like a huge stride up a sheer cliff. It was virtually impossible to put one foot in front of the other. The throbbing intensified. I wanted to talk but you have to be able to think to speak and my awareness was slipping, by the time I reached the corner, I had forgotten why I was there and even where I was. The pain in my head was so great I wanted to cry.

Stephens must have seen me. I had scaled the wall of the building and I was leaning on the stone garden wall, trying to get my breath back when I slumped to the ground. I remember Stephens putting his arms around me to try and support me and my body slipping through his fingers like water, my head still pulsated painfully. I remember feeling the damp soak through into my clothes, the feel of the cold hard pavement against my face, the hammering in my head. I remember closing my eyes and welcoming Morpheus as his arms opened. I was lost in his embrace. I was in oblivion and it was bliss.

My head still thumped with pain when I awoke in St Stephen's the next morning. Jo had convinced Stephens to take me there, saying we should call off the raid as the other officers there. I think she had concerns about my head. Stephens knew CID and reckoned they had made their arrests and taken one of the criminals off with them. Typically, they had left one behind.

Other Books We hope you have enjoyed the story. You might like to consider the following books by the same author:

Remember the Fifth November is the truth behind the Gunpowder Plot, Robert Catesby a convert to the Church of England was apparently a Catholic zealot, Robert Cecil with a spy network second to none failed to spot the movement of 36 barrels of gunpowder, how?

The Taint Gallery is a story of desire and betrayal set against a backdrop of contemporary London; this was love affair that led to deceit.

Switch, is a dark thriller, Chandler meets 'Fifty Shades of Grey'; a nightmare comes true.

Waterwitch is a sailing adventure: two brothers sailing a boat around the Mediterranean during the Falklands War, resulting in disastrous consequences.

Major Bruton's Safari or **Uganda Palaver** is a witty account of a coronation and a safari in Uganda.

As a guest of the Ugandan people, a group of disparate people experience Africa with a caustic commentator, not critical of the continent but of his own friends and family.

Innocent Proven Guilty is a thriller on the lines of 39 Steps. A teacher discovers his brother dead in a pool of blood, he wants to find the murderer but he has left his footprints behind

Seveny Seven is a 'Punk Portrait' The story of growing up in London during the punk era, a whimsical autobiography that explodes the myth that 'Punk' was an angry working class movement.

Carom is a thriller about an art theft and drug smuggling. Finn McHugh, and his team pursue Didier Pourchaire, a vicious art thief. The action moves between London, Paris, Helsinki and St. Petersburg. Everyone wants to catch the villain resulting in a messy bagatelle. Carom is an Indian board game.

Ad Bec is a dish best eaten cold; a schoolboy takes revenge on a bully. Stephen is a late arrival at a prep school in the depths of Shropshire.

He is challenged to do a 'tunnel dare' by the school bully. When the tunnel collapses on the bully, Stephen has to solve the dilemma, tell no one and be free or rescue the bully. The story is set in a seventies progressive preparatory school.

Karoly's Hungarian Tragedy is Michael's first departure into historical biography. This is the story of Karoly Ellenbacher taken into captivity and used as a human shield by Romanian soldiers during the war, arrested during the communist era and sent down a coal mine, he escaped to England in 1956. His story of survival is barely credible.

Michael Fitzalan has written four plays:

Veni, Vidi, Vicky, - is a story about a failed love affair.

George and the Dragon, a painter discovers a cache of bonds and sovereigns in a cellar, not knowing that it belongs to a vicious gang. Thankfully his niece's friend is a star lawyer and can help him return the money before it is too late, or can she?

Symposium for Severine is a modern version of Plato's Symposium but with women being the philosophers instead of men.

Superstar is a play that sees Thomas Dowting meeting Jesus in the Temple, travelling to Angel to meet his girlfriend Gabrielle. They convince Thomas to volunteer for work abroad. Three weeks later J C Goodman takes over Thomas's job and moves in with Gabrielle.

Switch and Major Bruton's Safari have been turned into scripts.

Michael is working on a script, which he may turn into a novel; *M.O.D, Mark O'Dwyer, Master of Disguise*, a private detective agency, Francis Barber Investigators, is retained to find out why a model was defenestrated from a Bond Street building.

23183229R00092

Printed in Poland
by Amazon Fulfillment
Poland Sp. z o.o., Wrocław